THE LEFT-HANDED DOLLAR

THE LEFT-HANDED DOLLAR

An Amos Walker Novel

Loren D. Estleman

A TOM DOHERTY ASSOCIATES BOOK
NEW YORK

THE LEFT-HANDED DOLLAR

Copyright © 2010 by Loren D. Estleman

Edited by James Frenkel

A Forge Book
Published by Tom Doherty Associates, LLC
175 Fifth Avenue
New York, NY 10010

www.tor-forge.com

Forge® is a registered trademark of Tom Doherty Associates, LLC.

ISBN 978-0-7653-1954-8

First Edition: December 2010

Printed in the United States of America

0 9 8 7 6 5 4 3 2 1

For Jamie and Robin Agnew, who make crime pay

THE LEFT-HANDED DOLLAR

ONE

L ucille Lettermore had a reputation for blindsiding prosecutors in court. She'd memorized the Michigan Penal Code and sprang up through loopholes to lash out at them unexpectedly in a kind of reverse Whack-a-Mole game.

Although she took on all sorts of clients, she preferred the unpopular ones: Communists, terrorists, Democrats, and other enemies of the social order. She'd spent more time behind bars on contempt charges than Koko the Giant Gorilla and had had her life threatened by people from every walk of society, including a Jesuit priest.

They called her Lefty Lucy.

I thought she was okay, but then I have a higher than average tolerance for lawyers. They account for 60 percent of my business.

We were in her office. "You look like a cable preacher," she said. "Your other suits are the kind I put on homeless clients to get them past the bailiff."

I thumbed a smooth gray lapel. I couldn't stop fondling the soft material. It was like trying to keep from running your hand over your first crew cut. "I lost three on my last job. I pooled the price and bought this one out of expenses. Something's bound to happen to it."

"Getting fatalistic in our extremity, are we?" But she wasn't really listening. Fashion meant nothing to her apart from what effect it might have on a jury. She wore her gray hair in bangs straight across the eyebrows and the rest to her collar, where she chopped it off like a broom. A pumpkin-colored blazer covered her linebacker's shoulders. People usually mistook her for a realtor.

"Anything on the platter at the moment?" she asked. "I include sleeper retainers, anything that might pull you off what you're working on."

"I committed to a bird feeder recently, but they can go to the park when I'm not home to fill it."

"Good, I need you exclusive. The homework alone on this one could take weeks."

"Who's the bankroll, William Clay Ford?"

"Joseph Michael Ballista. Know the name?"

"Joe Balls?"

"That was the old man. Try thinking more modern than the wartime black market. The Combination called him Joey Ballistic, partly because of his bad temper but mostly because he liked to blow things up. Allegedly," she added.

" 'The Combination.' " I grinned. "Now who's living in the past?"

"The Mafia, La Cosa Nostra, Radio Shack, the fucking Syndicate. Let's stay on topic. I'm burning off a deuce a minute in billable hours."

She never joked about that. She'd cleared all the law books off the shelves behind her and sold them to an interior decorator to make room for several dozen clocks, analog and digital, placed in her clients' direct line of sight to remind them that time was expensive and for Christ's sake get to the point. The decorator had had labels made with Shakespeare's titles embossed in gold to paste over the legal titles on the spines and stock the libraries of illiterate movie stars.

I said, "Sure, I remember Joey. I heard he died in the infirmary in Marion."

"You heard wrong. The Illinois quacks said he had cancer of the urinary tract and gave him six weeks to live. Then he passed a kidney stone and got better. The rich food they dish up in the federal system has made enough of those to build a new facility. He's back in Michigan now."

"Jackson?"

She shook her head. "He's out, sort of; rattling around his father's old barn in Bloomingham with an electronic tether on his ankle. I swung that, courtesy of the shitty financial situation in Lansing. Prisoners are high-maintenance, and old-fashioned gangsters seem cuddly since Nine-Eleven. He poses no threat."

Bloomingham is Detroitspeak for the tony communities of Birmingham, West Bloomfield, and Bloomfield Village, where they cut the grass with Norelcos and hand out gold American Express cards at Halloween. Once they started letting in retired county executives it had been only a matter of time before the underworld set up housekeeping there.

"He wasn't always harmless," I said.

"Water over the dam. This time they're trying him for uttering and publishing. A bad-check rap after all those years on J. Edgar's hit parade."

"They got Capone on tax evasion."

"You're regressing further. With his priors it's a life sentence. The man's paid his debt."

"Probably with a bum check."

"It's a frame. Somebody else in the Com—the organization signed someone else's name using his penmanship, a double forgery. Joey was on parole, so back he goes to serve out the rest of his original sentence on a conviction for illegal possession of a blackjack. Hell's sake, if he didn't pick up the habit in stir he'd never have survived his first incarceration."

"Representing a hoodlum is almost respectable for you."

We were in her office in the old National Bank Building five stories above the demented carousel of automobiles, pedestrians, and traffic barricades that is Cadillac Square. The walls were painted an eye-watering apple green and hung with photographs in transparent frames of Lucille at various ages and dress sizes, taking up space with Bobby Seale, Father Charles Coughlin, Jane Fonda, Michael Moore or Meatloaf, and Roman Polanski. Judging by collar types and the breadth of Polanski's necktie, they'd posed for that one about the time he fled the U.S. to avoid standing trial for statutory rape. That complaint was long past the age of consent, but he was still making movies in Europe and the bailbondsman Lucille had recommended was still blackening her name all over the Internet. The FBI had leased an outside storage unit to contain her file.

She shifted her impressive weight around in her orange leather chair and crossed a pair of plump ankles under the sheet of plate glass she used for a desk. "The state attorney general's people know it's a frame, that goes without saying. I stop short of suggesting they arranged it, but I'm entitled to my suspicions. The last A.G. didn't stay long enough to warm the seat before hopping into the governor's mansion. Considering how well that turned out, this one needs a boost."

"Isn't it unethical for one member of your profession to bad-mouth another outside court?"

"Ethics is a loser's word."

"So get him off."

"I wouldn't know where to start. You can stir up all kinds of shit when you're standing in it; I wrote the book on that. But I've never represented a client I thought wasn't guilty.

"It's an interesting moral dilemma," she finished.

I felt like smoking over that one. I showed her the pack, brows lifted.

"The building's gone nonsmoking. Open the window." When I hesitated she said, "I put in some time on the tobacco companies' legal team."

"Wasn't that antiproletariat?"

"I turned in my party card under Jimmy Carter. The tobacco settlement paid pennies to the victims and billions to the slush fund. It was all about money from the start, just like everything else."

I'd have expected a lawyer to have known that, but the most idealistic man I'd ever met had served ninety days for procurement. He never got over being arrested after the cop had told him point blank he wasn't a cop. I got up and tugged open the window, releasing into the room a puff of fetid air, carrying that molasses-and-urine stink of midday downtown baking in the sun. A city bus carrying more advertising than passengers waddled through the intersection and sighed against the curb, trading one customer on a walker for another.

I threw a match into the column of heat and trailed smoke back to my chair. "Make a deal. Joey probably overheard them setting up the Bugsy Siegel hit when he was in the womb."

"The A.G.'s people offered one, with a fed chaser: immunity in return for his testimony against some of his old friends. Parole restrictions lifted and witness protection, the same old horseshit in the same old sack. I said no dice."

"Run it past your client?"

"The American Bar Association insists upon it."

"That's not an answer."

"You worry about your ticket, I'll worry about mine." She changed the subject. "I don't usually explain myself, but you and I have clocked a lot of miles, and I gave up keeping score on who steered more business whose way. The truth is I got mad when RICO passed, with its provisions for setting aside the Bill of Rights to put racketeers behind bars. It was an admission of failure on the good guys' part, that the law couldn't punish lawbreakers without breaking the law itself. I've won some and I've lost more, but never by default."

I tapped ash into a pants cuff and listened. I'd had to fight the tailor to have it.

"Those blow-dried neo-Stalinists in the Justice Department expect me to play by their rules, even when they don't," she said. "I won't. I'm going to swipe Joey right out from under their noses. They moved into my weight class when they made him an underdog."

"One with millions in unreported income. Nice doggie."

"I soak 'em when they got it. How about you?"

"I got third-degree burns out of the last."

She uncrossed her ankles and laid a pair of Popeye fore-
arms on the desk. From three feet away I could smell the
coffee on her breath; I think she chewed the grounds when
the water was too slow. "Anyway," she said, "what chance
does a character like him stand hiding out in some cornfield
in Kansas? He'd be as inconspicuous as a pinky ring at a
tent revival."

"What's your game plan?"

"So glad you asked." She counted on her fingers. "That
blackjack conviction's a joke; if I'd been his attorney then
I'd have made the case for a plant, and I can get that decision reversed by sweating the right people. The federal
takedown came from lying to the FBI; apart from the fact
that no one gives a shit, Justice's star witness tainted his
testimony when he got slapped with community service for
perjuring himself on one point during cross, and I can land
Joey a new trial on that alone. My guess is they'll drop the
charge to avoid embarrassment, but if they're pigheaded
enough to go through with it I'll wipe my ass with their case
in court. See where I'm headed?"

"I'd rather not, but you draw too clear a picture."

Actually I'd begun to understand. I went over to the window and watched what was left of my cigarette trace spirals
down to the sidewalk, then turned my back on it and stuck
my hands in my pockets. "Didn't he bribe an official to put
him on a work-release program back in Jackson? He got
another sentence for that and the official drew unemploy-
ment."

"I'm shedding big fat greasy tears for the official, inside.
I'll squeeze them back out if he decides to sue and retains
me. Right now we're talking about Joey. If he shouldn't

have been in jail in the first place, the circumstances are extenuating. New trial: See above."

"He's just Snow White, isn't he? Only he isn't. The judge sent him to Jackson for attempted murder. He wired a bundle of dynamite to the ignition of some chump's car and blew off the chump's leg."

"That's the keystone of my strategy. If I can swing a Mulligan and win him an acquittal, the bribery case goes away. With the other two bits expunged, I'll plead no contest on the bad-check charge and petition the judge to sentence him as a first offender. He'll be released for time served." She sat back beaming. Lucille Lettermore wearing a smile was like a Great White picking its teeth.

"Congratulations. A born-again virgin's a tough sell, but if it can be sold you're the girl."

"Not without help. You've been a detective almost as long as Joey's been in trouble. I have to assume you've learned a thing or two in all that time. I want you to find the evidence that will set aside that first conviction and help put an innocent man back on the street."

"Pass."

"Why, because he's a thug?"

"I've spent enough time with them to catch sports-shirt poisoning, but there's a cure for that. I'm not as good as you think."

"Bullshit. Shit of the bull." She had a fecal fetish. "What's eating you, really?"

I lit another, as long as I was standing next to the ashtray. There was nothing for it but to pin my heart on my new worsted sleeve. "That chump Joey blew up in his car? He's my only friend."

TWO

You'll be glad you agreed to come along," she said. "He's not the punk he used to be. Those years in and out of institutions changed him."

"If they didn't change his DNA, I'm not interested. You're paying me to take a ride, not for my good opinion of Joey Ballistic."

"I'd shitcan the nickname. He's unreasonable about it."

"Right. No sense lighting his fuse."

We were heading north on Telegraph Road in the mauve Volvo station wagon Lucille had been driving for twenty years. I think she'd acquired it with just a few thousand miles on the clock from a client who wouldn't be needing it for three to five years, in lieu of her fee. She maintained it with all the care of a woman who had no time for pets or children, no personal life worth talking about; we had that in common if little else. The clock had turned over a couple of times and all she'd had to replace was the battery, brakes, and tires. The unbroken string of Best Buys, Targets, Home Depots, and PetSmarts on each side of the eight-lane highway slid its oily reflection over six coats of Turtle Wax on the hood.

"You and Barry Stackpole have a real history," she said.

"If I had a bottle of Scotch as old as our history I'd save it for my wedding day."

Barry and I had shared a shell hole under enemy fire, a dozen cases of strong spirits, and mutually beneficial information over a period that had outlasted most marriages, not counting one long dry spell when we weren't speaking. I'd been an MP at the start, he a correspondent with *Stars and Stripes*, and we hadn't wandered far from the gate. In my case an experiment in organized law enforcement had led to the disorganized variety I was still practicing, while Barry had parlayed a spot on *The Detroit News* police beat into a syndicated column, then a cable TV show, and finally a Web site that news and police agencies alike paid to download information on criminal activity the world over. Back on the *News*, he'd been too preoccupied ducking a subpoena to testify to a grand jury investigating the old Combination to pop the hood of his Chevy Impala and see the explosive charge that had taken the car, one of his legs, two fingers, and a saucer-size piece of his skull when he turned the key.

"Joey was just a button back then," I told Lucille, as if I'd been talking right along instead of just remembering. "Even the old man was only a subcapo or something, with a vending machine route and a cathouse on Michigan Avenue. That bit Joey did for attempted murder was the turning point for them both. He did it standing up, not naming names, and when he got out, his father was in charge of the Guerrera brothers' old outfit and made Joey his lieutenant. That put him in line for boss when the old man died."

"Not counting a few vacations courtesy of the local and federal authorities." Lucille drove with her hands at ten and two, a couple of miles under the limit in the slow lane with everyone passing her. Her reputation for recklessness didn't extend to the road. "Detroit cops fitted him to a partial print on the wad of chewing gum the dynamiter used to paste down the wires. I'm pretty sure the lab rat fudged on the number of points of resemblance when he took the stand, but you can't sweat a dead man, and the forensics report is water stained beyond legibility. They ought to fix the fucking roof at Thirteen Hundred instead of juicing up the riverfront for tourists." Detroit Police Headquarters, an eighty-year-old landmark at 1300 Beaubien, was alternately scheduled for renovation and demolition, with no change in the situation of the uniforms and plainclothes detectives dodging drips and rotten floorboards. "A chemical test will settle the point if I can get my hands on that piece of gum."

"Yuck."

"All they had to go on back then was blood types," she said. "Every new weapon in the war on crime is another nail in the coffin of sloppy police work."

"What's stopping you?" We'd left the strip malls behind and were gliding past tree plantings and upscale restaurants, breathing the bottled-in-bond air of the Bloomies. Names of lakes had replaced the mile numbers on the road signs and suburban prowl cars squatted on the median, looking for broken taillights and patches of rust and similar evidence of invasion from the city to the south.

"Not stopping me, boyo; just slowing me down. The system, what else? They store the evidence separate from the paperwork, and somebody lost it. I figure it's stuck to the chief's bedpost."

"It could've been honestly misplaced. It's been years and years. DPD isn't Scotland Yard."

"Scotland *Yard* isn't Scotland Yard. I put in farmout work for a firm of London solicitors over the Official Secrets Act over there. The dumb fucks in Washington have nothing on those tweedy inspectors when it comes to trying to find their asses with both hands." She gunned the Volvo through an intersection a split second before the light turned yellow. I don't think we caught one red that whole trip. In addition to being a careful driver, Lucille was a very good one, with a course at the Bondurant school of race driving on her lengthy resumé. She'd foiled a kidnap try, or maybe just an attempt to scare her, by doubling back on her pursuer long enough to catch the number on his plate before disengaging. There's no law against following someone one time, but the cops had paid a visit and there had been no more such incidents. Her enemies had fallen back on the usually reliable practice of bribing someone to challenge her license, but she'd survived that, too. She was the beep-beep-Roadrunner of defense lawyers.

She said, "I'm bragging, not complaining. They're afraid of me or they'd have come up with something more original than the old shell game. I've filed with Freedom of Information, but that takes too long. I expect one of my snitches to come through anytime. If the Man were serious about putting the kibosh on me, he'd raise the salaries of his civil servants. I'm their annuity."

"So why the offer? I've got almost as much bad blood

against me in the system as you, and a hell of a lot fewer re-
sources."

"Because I dot all the *i*'s and cross all the *t*'s, and when
I've dotted and crossed them all, I make up some more.
You're a pit bull, Amos, just like me. If they flush that piece
of gum, you'll find something maybe not as good, but good
enough to sweat out whoever flushed it, and I'll swing a new
trial on prima facie. There's never just one smoking gun.
When they're this committed, there's usually an arsenal."

"You're counting too heavily on me changing my mind.
I don't get as many jobs as I need, but I need the friends
I've got more."

"You can always make new friends. There are three hundred million Americans now. Your odds are improving by
the day."

There was no use arguing that point. She had no friends
that I knew of, but work enough to keep her mind off the
fact. She was like the multimillionaire who said money
wasn't important.

"I'm talking about justice," she went on; "small *j*. It de-
serves the capital, but those crumbs in Washington have
pissed all over it just like everything else."

I looked at her, at her bulldog profile against the greenery
and wrought-iron skidding past the window on her side.
"Do you really buy that, or is it just another one of your notorious summations to the jury?"

"Honey, I was sold when I passed the Bar. Don't you
think I could be rich enough to bankroll Bill Gates if I'd offered my considerable services to a corporation? I'm not
talking about Big Tobacco; they were going down for the

third time when I joined their team. Someone has to look out for the Rule of Law when it's out of favor."

There was a philosophical discussion there, if we'd had the time, but my Plato was rusty, and she'd slowed for the turn onto Squirrel Lake Road, where the gin joints and roadhouses of the giddy postwar world had gone to the wrecking ball and baronial estates had sprung up on their foundations. We sprayed gravel on the apron of a private road named for Joseph Michael Ballista's Castellammarise mother's family and followed it to a turnaround in front of the rambling Tudor mansion that Joe Balls had had built by Old World stonemasons and carpenters on four acres wooded with American walnut trees, with a clear-cut circle around it designed to discourage assassins from seeking cover during assaults on the ancestral estate. There was just enough wind to keep the plywood sawyer in the front yard busy gnawing at his log; never underestimate the capacity of the newly rich to junk up a piece of residential real estate.

I stood with her in front of a sheltered panel door while she waited for someone to answer the chimes: They seemed to be ringing out the theme to *The Sound of Music*, but it might have been Puccini. There's not much room for nuance when just four metal tubes are involved in the performance. In due course of time, the summons was answered by an East Indian houseboy in a white coat with gold frogs, and we measured out a portion of mortality while the manservant excused himself to see if the master of the house was in residence.

"As if he could get more than five hundred feet outside the door without alerting the constabulary," Lucille said.

We heard him stumping for a while before he entered the foyer, which was as bare of furniture as if he were moving out. He came in leaning on a cane with a faux ivory grip poured into the shape of a leaping fish. There are various degrees of being sixty, and you can look like forty if you take care of yourself and the genes are sound, but neither of those circumstances was present in Joey Ballistic's case. The leg he needed the cane for ended in a gnarled root of an appendage in a white sock in a sandal, and the pain of the gout that throbbed there had drawn the blood from his face and the color from his scant hair. Deep gullies in his features made him a twin of his father in his last days. Those were fifteen years in the past, caused by complications from syphillis, the disease that sought out gangsters the way lung cancer stalked Hollywood.

"Counselor." His lips peeled back from shockingly white veneers and he changed hands on the cane to grasp hers. "Hope you brought a pair of bolt cutters. This thing itches like a case of crabs." He waggled his good foot in a soft Italian leather loafer with the bulge of the tether showing just above the spot where the cuff of his trousers broke at the instep.

"When the time comes, I'll have the attorney general take it off himself. Joe, meet Amos Walker. I'm hoping to assign him to investigate your case."

He turned a pair of eyes on me with no more shine to them than petrified black walnuts. But I saw a dull glimmer of recognition. "Frankie Acardo; *long* time ago. You tried to warn him the Colombians were laying for him."

"I didn't try all that hard." His memory impressed me. Except for grudges, his kind didn't encourage the faculty.

"His old man Jackie partnered with my father for a little. Dumb as fireplugs, Jackie *and* Frankie. Frankie's Uncle Tommy was the brains of that family. Somebody shoved him over the side of one of his own quarries and spilled them all over the bottom."

"Good times."

I felt the woman at my side stiffen, but we were spared the awkwardness of his offering his hand and my not shaking it. His face went as dead as his eyes. Then he showed the dentalwork again, like fresh plaster on a condemned building, and turned to lead us into the bowels of the house, changing hands again on the cane to get all the good out of it.

His saggy body wore a vintage-looking yellow sports shirt tail out over tan poplin slacks, with a wide vertical brown stripe on either side of the placket. The silk suits almost never come out any more exept at weddings, christenings, and the weekly funeral. Casual wear is the uniform of Las Vegas, their real Vatican.

Lucille had called the place Joe Balls's barn. It was as empty as one before the harvest. Our footsteps on the marble and ceramic rustled among the exposed oak beams high above our heads. In the old days, I'd heard, the shining time between Batista's rise to power in Cuba and the police raid on Apalachin, the rooms had been packed with Grecian urns, Deco panels, Impressionist paintings, Turkish rugs, Japanese screens, and medieval European armor, a woozy compost that made visitors stagger as if they'd been mixing beer with port and malt whisky with applejack. Then Joey's mother passed (a suicide, some said), and Joseph Senior's gray cells began to spoil while the gorillas in the board-room discussed whether to let nature take its course or make a call before he babbled all he knew about Albert Anastasia, Jimmy Hoffa, and the grassy knoll. He'd died awaiting a decision and Joseph Junior auctioned everything off and went minimal. FBI listening devices were getting smaller and smaller and there was no point in providing so many places to hide them.

No doubt the ephemeral quality of Joey's freedom had led to more yard sales, with his wife separated from him by legal decree and a county line, and no one else to enjoy the comforts for long stretches. Or maybe he favored the open space after a nine by twelve cell. In any case the walk seemed longer than it was and awakened the agoraphobe in me.

We came to a stop finally in a completely furnished room: plush chairs with worn arms, low tables with ashtrays, a bleeding heart in a frame, and the smell of expensive cigars. Wine glittered in a spinsterish old decanter on the dropleaf of a maple secretary with a few books on the shelves, thumb-worn long ago, titled in Italian; neither he nor his father had seen fit to add to a library that had come over with Joey's grandfather from Sicily when the first Roosevelt was in the White House.

He poured himself wine, diluting it with water from a less ornate container, a concession to gout, and sat without offering us any of either, propping his foot on a hassock and hooking his cane over an arm of the chair. When Lucille and I sat down I caught him watching me curiously, as if having placed the name he might remember where he'd seen the man.

He wouldn't. The only time we'd been face-to-face he'd been standing on the wrong side of a one-way mirror, when I wheeled Barry Stackpole into a police lineup room to identify him.

THREE

Someone, maybe the houseboy, had stuck a birdhouse on a pole in a patch of watered lawn visible through a French door (in a Tudor house; there should be a three-day waiting period before hiring an architect), where a cardinal perched on a peg checked the place for suspicious wires. I reminded myself to pick up seed for my feeder on the way home. If it was intended to take Joey's mind off his years in the joint, it was a waste of effort, because he sat with his back to it. He was a city squirrel.

"I don't guess you got in to see the governor," he told Lucille. "The old man wanted me to go into politics. Maybe if I listened I'd be in line for a pardon."

"I'm waiting for a callback. I don't overlook much."

"That count the deal they offered?"

She waited in silence. She'd had too much practice not reacting to surprises in court to give him satisfaction.

He looked at me, cradling the glass in both hands. "They want to send me someplace so different from here no one'll think to look for me there. What's the opposite of Detroit?"

"Bisbee."

"Bisbee, what's that?"

"Little town in Arizona, near the Mexican border. The Clantons hung out there when they weren't trading bullets with the Earps and Doc Holliday."

"And that's opposite how?"

I thought. "The tamales are better."

Lucille said, "You should lend me your sources. I've been shuttling back and forth between here and Lansing, burning up the wires to Washington, turning over turf looking for witnesses, and you know as much as I do just sitting here swilling chianti."

"French burgundy. Dago red gives me the Tuscan Two-Step. Did you think I'd take the deal if you told me about it?"

"Do you think you could sit around drinking French burgundy and watching ESPN in New Mexico or someplace and not get the bright idea to skim off an Indian casino?"

"What're you, an injun lover?"

"Sit around feeding your gout in Seattle and not try selling protection to Japanese restaurants?"

"You got something—"

"Sit around twirling that stick in New Orleans and not cut yourself a slice of the graft? Do anything that won't draw old enemies like maggots to shit?"

He understood then. Somehow I hadn't thought he ever would. There's a rumor making the rounds that if certain notorious ganglords would apply their genius to legitimate enterprise, the country would be up to its neck in Donald Trumps, but the people responsible for the rumor had never spent time with the mob. Legislate Wal-Mart out of the competition and the Rain Man could show profit.

"All I'm saying is you should've told me." It sounded like a whine.

"I wanted to avoid this conversation. I'll do everything I can to shield you from the system. Protecting you from yourself is a massive waste of billable hours."

He sought distraction from the lecture and found it in me. "She said she's hoping to assign you to my case. What's it take to measure up to your standards?"

"You can't afford it," I said.

"Name a figure."

"I can name nine. Eight dead, onc crippled."

"I get it. When was I ever convicted of killing anybody? When was I charged?"

I got up, poured a glass of wine, looked at Lucille, who shook her head. I brought it back to my chair. "I don't care about the eight. They were in the business, knew the risks. Stackpole did, too, but he wasn't in the business. That makes all the difference. He didn't trust the system any more than you do; if they'd put him on the stand, he'd have sat out a contempt charge at County until the grand jury's term expired rather than make the system the beneficiary of all his work and risk. Well, you didn't ask him. Ever since then he's been hobbling around on a Dutch leg with a glove on one hand like Michael Jackson and a tin patch on his head."

"You know Stackpole?"

"They're friends," his lawyer said. "It's a question of conflict of interest."

"I wasn't in that."

"Sure," I said. "That's your ticket out, if you can convince an appellate court judge."

"I wasn't in it."

"You didn't say that then. You stood mute at your arraignment and stayed that way until they let you out. There was a real future to be gained from the time investment, with the Combination. You even got a nickname: Joey Ballistic. You can't buy that kind of PR, you have to earn it. Now you want to rewind and start over. I guess the good life isn't so hot in blue denims."

"You've worn 'em, too."

That surprised me, though I hoped I was as good as Lucille at covering it. I had a small reputation—not small enough, it seemed, to escape the attention of a class I had no interest in attracting. He knew me, all right; I just didn't know from where. It put me at a serious disadvantage and he knew it.

He drank from his glass and let a scarlet drop quiver on his lip while he fixed me with his black-walnut gaze. His skin was jaundiced, nearly the same shade of orange as his attorney's blazer, with cigarette-ash gray in the hollows; that pruno they brew in prison toilets turns kidneys to rice pudding and swells livers to the size of gourds. He was the unhealthiest-looking man I'd ever seen outside ICU, and the circles I traveled in weren't known for their fitness routines. Freedom for him would be brief, interrupted by midnight trips to emergency rooms and days spent listening to his own urine trickling into plastic bags, until they drew the respirator from his throat and shut down the equipment. I didn't pity him, just the sordid fate of the brotherhood of mortal man.

"I never killed a man I wasn't looking in the eye."

I waited a couple of ticks before I took a sip of wine; sickly sweet stuff, with an aftertaste of Penzoil. You never see a thug at tastings, but the houseboy or whoever stocked his cellar had taken liberties. It did nothing to lift my sudden fit of depression. One of the curses of the life that has pressed itself upon me is I always know when someone is telling me the truth.

"You're taking the job." Lucille shifted lanes to give the road to a shift worker who rode bumpers to get back to whatever was waiting for him at home. I had a flock of disgruntled birds and the mammals who spent their nocturnal hours figuring out how to beat the system. I was in no such hurry.

"Did I say I was taking it?"

"You didn't have to. You forget I've made a nice living out of reading jurors. You're convinced he's innocent."

"They ought to strike that word from the dictionary."

"If I waited for a client who could pose for a Precious Moments billboard, I'd be spending most of my time chasing ambulances. No matter what else he's done—"

"He's done plenty."

"No matter what else he's done," she pounded on, "it doesn't give the attorney general and his cronies in the District a wild card to clear their books just to make room for another entry. Better to let a hundred guilty men go free—"

"I've heard the anthem. Clearing Joey won't put the real perp at the defendant's table. There's a statute of limitations on attempted murder."

"If Stackpole's truly dedicated to setting the record straight, that won't matter."

I didn't address that. She'd spent too much time in courtrooms, where the jury knew less about the case under consideration than the channel-surfing public. It was one of the requirements of being seated.

"Where will you start?"

"I need expenses. I spent the discretionary fund on toothpaste."

"Open the glove compartment."

There was a No. 10 envelope inside with my name written on it in her splashy hand. It contained a cashier's check for fifteen hundred, my standard retainer. It didn't cheer me up. "I hate being a foregone conclusion." I put the check in my wallet.

"I don't make any other kind. What else do you need?"

"A look at the police file, including the forensics report. An original, if you can manage it. I might be able to make something of the part that got smudged."

She took a hand off the wheel, reached behind the seats toward the back floorboard, and slung a fat ten-by-fourteen manila envelope onto my lap.

"Good luck with that. I paid a chemist a bundle to come up with a solvent that makes those blackouts on FBI files go away, but that shit that drips from ceilings is what carved the Grand Canyon. I threw in the report filed by the investigators I hired," she added. "You know the firm, I think. Reliance?"

"You should've stuck with them. They've got equipment and manpower. I've got an envelope." I undid the clasp and lifted the flap. A sour stench of neglected laundry rolled out. I resealed it before the odor got into her upholstery. The car smelled pleasantly of leather briefcases.

"Too establishment. Ernie Krell got his license under

LBJ. When you've been around that long and government security contracts start coming in regular as Netflix, you fall into the habit of sharing information. They're okay for the broad strokes, but you need a maverick when it comes to finish work. Staying one after twenty years takes work and concentration. I know my species when I see it."

"Mavericks aren't a species. They're stray cows. They spend most of their time trying to keep from getting butchered."

"Keeps 'em alert."

She stopped for a light finally, one she could have beaten. Now that the question of the day was settled she seemed to have uncoiled a little. "The arresting officer's still alive. Veteran of the old racket squad. Took a buyout a dozen or so years ago, operates a marina and sells sporting equipment on Portage Lake. Know the place?"

"I'll find it. I'm a detective." Sporting equipment meant guns. I'd hoped I wouldn't have to arm myself on a cold case.

"There's still plenty of light, and it's his big season. You should find him in a mellow mood." She was in her mind-reading phase.

"In the morning, when most of his customers are at work," I said. "I have to see someone else first."

"Stackpole? You don't need his permission."

"No, but I need mine."

The conversation fell off after that. The light changed, we turned east, and in a little while I was unlocking the door of my haggard Cutlass and tossing Joey Ballistic's case history into the passenger's side. In the heat through the windshield the interior smelled like an old truck cab.

"I hope that heap has an alarm." She sat idling at the curb, an elbow resting on her window ledge. "I can be disbarred just for letting an original police report outside the system."

"Thieves go around banging on parked cars looking for alarms. That's how they know there's something inside worth stealing." I punched down the peg and slammed the door. "I'll be in touch, progress or no."

"Not if no. At my rates I can't afford small talk." She put the car in gear.

I jacked some coins into the meter and took a stroll. It was too nice a day to drive a couple of blocks and there was no telling how long it would be before another space opened downtown. I don't know where the people go who park in them. If the sidewalks were any less crowded you could grow corn in the cracks.

Apartments were one suggestion. Things are looking up there, away from the spreading dry rot of the neighbor-hoods and in spite of the open money drain that leads straight from the casinos to Nevada. Blitzed property val-ues make for affordable rent, and cash left over to sandblast the gang graffiti off brick and stone, replace leprous fire es-capes with Venetian balconies, and lure the third generation of refugees back from suburbia. For the first time in the city's three-hundred-year history, flats threaten to outnum-ber one-family houses. The residents tend to be designers of computer games and builders of Web sites, people who can work anywhere because they work at home for cus-tomers far outside the Detroit area, where the Industrial Revolution has been lost. Glasses, pimples, and Famous Monsters of Filmland T-shirts are shoving out business suits and coveralls. It all has the appearance of life, but an eerie quality, too, because of the location, as if Greenwich Village had moved to Manhattan Midtown. It's cosmetics, like nice white teeth in the mouth of a decaying gangster.

Barry Stackpole, capping a long nomadic existence spent skipping from one temporary address to another like bin Laden, had taken a long-term lease at last on a second-story apartment two blocks north of Lucille Lettermore's building. The world had turned; the Sicilian Super Friends were too busy sandbagging themselves against the tide from the Racketeer Influenced and Corrupt Organizations act to tack targets on whistle-blowing reporters, and the bounty on his head had expired years ago. I'd put him on to the place after a murder was committed there, which gave him a break on the rent. Some Detroiters are leary about things like that.

I'd come to regret it. The place had bad memories.

I went past the elevator and climbed a stairwell that had been repainted in recent months. The smell was bright and crisp, like bubblegum. It would take another year for the memory of tobacco spit and sweaty icemen and bathtub gin to worry through two coats of latex. That was the kind of traffic the steps had attracted in the building's department-store days, with its lifts and wooden escalators for the patrons.

The Edwardian bowl fixtures in the hallway ceiling, outside the old business offices, had been ripped out and replaced with fluorescents, which in turn had been scrapped in favor of new bowl fixtures made to look like the originals, only more expensive and of poorer quality. I stopped before the brass numerals on Barry's door, knocked twice, got no answer. No sound came from inside. His working hours were filled with the cartoon noises that junk up the Net.

I unshipped my no-frills cell phone and dialed his number. I heard the recorded announcement in stereo, in my ear and from the other side of the door: "I'm on assignment. Call back." No beep followed. Sources who would take a chance on leaving a message weren't the kind that he encouraged. I climbed back down.

FOUR

During the February doldrums, when only the rusty brown of the snow brings color to Michigan, I'd mounted a feeder on my solitary tree to attract goldfinches and cardinals. By spring it had begun to attract squirrels as well, so I'd bought a pole, put the feeder on top, and cut off the limb I'd hung it from to discourage the rodents from scampering along it and dropping onto the feeder from above. I'd underestimated their gymnastic skills; the seeds were gone every morning, proving that it's possible for a creature that measures ten inches from nose to tail to bound a dozen feet straight out from the trunk, execute a triple somersault, and land straight up in the middle of a feast.

I bought a box of three-inch spikes and drove them through the roof of the feeder with the points facing up, an iron maiden effect more psychological than physical. The assaults continued. One morning, standing at the kitchen window drinking coffee, I watched a medium-size gray squirrel shinny up the pole from the ground. That led to my adding a fat slick stovepipe to the pole, which worked until the night something dug the pole out of the ground and dumped it over on its side.

"Raccoon," said the Animal Control officer I got on the telephone. "Squirrels aren't that smart. Coons are problem solvers. What you want to do is trap them. Can't shoot 'em in the city." He sounded resigned to the fact.

The live box trap I bought caught a seriously disgruntled black squirrel, which I loaded, trap and all, into my trunk and drove out to a wooded area in the suburbs and set free. It hopped into the underbrush without a rearward glance.

The next day I found the trap turned upside down and the hatch open; something much bigger than a squirrel had managed to overturn it and let gravity do the rest. I borrowed a jack handle from the Cutlass and inserted it through the holes in the cage to anchor the trap to the earth. I found a sullen raccoon inside it the following morning, as big as a terrier. It tore up the carpet in the trunk and made a mad dash for freedom when I let it out in the wooded lot.

Two squirrels and a raccoon and a half later (the adolescent looked cuddly, but just missed sinking a fang into my hand when I tipped up the hatch before it took flight), I called Animal Control again and listened to twenty minutes of *Dr. Dolittle* before a voice came on, different from the first. "You want to call a private service," this one said.

"What've they got that you don't?"

"Manpower. The city tossed a coin and it came down on catching murderers."

Critter-B-Gone sent a man who paced off my lawn and used the onboard computer in his prison van to estimate a hundred dollars to erect an electric fence. I said, "All this started with a ten-dollar feeder and three bucks' worth of millet. Now I'm thinking of taking out a second mortgage. What else you got?"

"Tranquilizer darts; but you can't afford 'em. No one can. It means paying a man to stake out the place all night and, believe me, you got more raccoons than we got men."

"What guarantee can you give me on the electric fence?"

"You'll fry one or two. The rest'll just dig under."

"Someone must be able to afford something. I see feeders all over and not a rooftop sniper in sight."

He smiled wearily. He had a long, humorous, tired face under a Tigers away cap with a horseshoe brim. "If anyone could it's Aretha Franklin. The soul singer? She's got all the money in the world and the worst critter problem in three counties. It's like they painted a target on her house."

I had a premonition. "Where's she live?"

"Up in the 'burbs. Plenty of woods."

I resolved to find another refuge for my wildlife.

The morning after I met with Lucille Lettermore, I used a spade to build a berm around the base of the feeder, then drank coffee and smoked over the Reliance Investigations report. Randolph Severin, the detective who'd put the cuffs on Joseph Ballista for the Stackpole bombing, hadn't let any grass grow under his feet before he lit out with his retirement cash to Portage Lake, one of a chain of bodies of freshwater held together by Livingston County, and sunk it in a marina. Michigan registers more boats than any other state, but most of them spend their time on the shoreline of the Great Lakes. Livingston was still wilderness then, and the investment would have fallen within the modest means of a career cop who'd taken early buyout.

Much had changed since. Detroit continued to empty out,

and real estate in the wealthier suburbs had priced itself out of the budgets of the middle bracket. Speculators had moved northwest, turned roadside vegetable stands and rustic vacation cabins into chain stores and McMansions, and soaked the desperate hordes from the southeast hundreds of thousands on the dollar for the privilege of commuting three hours round-trip to make the money they needed to keep up the mortgages. Catering to the waterborne carriage trade, Severin stood to have recouped his original stake many times over, provided he hadn't drunk it up early.

I was hoping he had. I stopped at the bank to cash my check and put some in my wallet to prime the pump.

I tried Barry's number again from the road and got the machine again. An overnight assignment might mean hair extensions, a three-day beard, and a Brooklyn accent. He got around his disabilities on undercover duty not by concealing them, but by emphasizing them, with wheelchairs and walkers and a clumsy prosthetic hand that suggested he'd lost more than two lousy fingers. The thought was encouraging. Cloak-and-dagger detail usually put him in a good mood. From the start he'd preferred to work the field and let someone back home splice his infinitives and reel in his participles.

I was dressed for the lake country, in a navy sports shirt, gray flannels, and deck shoes showing wear. While the tank was filling I popped the nifty little hatch below my glove compartment to check the Chief's Special and speedloader for shells. I considered clipping the revolver to my belt under my shirttail, but a police background is a chronic thing; if Severin sold guns, he'd know all the tells, and you only get one chance to make a good first impression.

The day was made for rusticating. A brutal winter had obliterated spring, followed by a summer on the good old order, with a Crayola sun on a construction-paper sky and half-naked sunbathers sprouting on the roofs of student housing. School was out, but the nicer the weather, the lighter the exodus home to cut grass and clean gutters. Laid-off line workers sat on front porches in their undershirts, sucking on longnecks at eight A.M., nursing their grievances, and waiting for their big break on *Cops*. In Detroit there's something for everyone between Memorial Day and the Labor Day blowout.

I entered I-96, the Jeffries, against the tidal flow of traffic from the west. In a little while the barbed wire and billboards thinned out and the miniature Great Walls began, shutting out housing developments from the whistle of tires on the interstate. An odd farmhouse or barn sprang up in the spaces between, with a bulldozer in its future. You wondered where they expected to grow the ethanol. Farther along, trees grew in clumps like broccoli, in squares of evergreens for sale at Christmastime, then in straight rows along the apron, where members of the local deer population stained the pavement with their blood. Orange plastic barrels crowded out traffic lanes, braided westbound with eastbound past portable concrete dividers to keep the strands from colliding head-on, and signs warned of fines and jail time for running over construction workers, but we were all going too fast to read them. We never slowed down except to stop for bottlenecks or to let some piece of grubby yellow equipment cross. Half-finished overpasses made apostrophes against the sky. It will be a pretty state when they get it finished.

At Howell, home of the Ku Klux Klan and the annual melon festival, I traded the expressway for a winding two-lane blacktop where the scenery restored my faith in country stores and schools not surrounded by chain link, where imperturbable rabbits munched on blue lupine without even pricking their ears at the close proximity of wheels. I'd been dead wrong about Bisbee, Arizona. The opposite of Detroit is only a tank of gas away.

The village of Pinckney greeted me with a scent of tuberose and Unguentine; someone had laid it between tissues sometime around the Bay of Pigs. I pulled onto a patch of baked asphalt in front of a corner market to confer with a county map. That led me to another serpentine stretch of blacktop past more trees and shards of blue water flashing between the trunks. I turned left after a couple of country blocks and crept along a line of shaded cottages separated by manmade canals connected to a broad expanse of lake until I came to a sign pegged into a patch of crushed limestone with yellow lightbulbs stuttering all around the edge:

RANDY'S MARINA
Boats for Sale and Rent
Boating Equipment
Snowmobiles
Camping Supplies

A long low building with chalky white siding and a privy roof stood at the end of a downward-sloping driveway with a 1970 Ford pickup parked off to one side and next to it a new van with a satellite dish mounted on top. A row of ca-

noes and kayaks leaned against the long wall, chained together like convicts through loops on their sterns. What
I assumed to be the advertised snowmobiles slumbered
under a tarpaulin tied with Gordian bowlines to iron rings
sunk in a concrete pad, awaiting their season. SPORTING
EQUIPMENT SOLD HERE, read a faded banner stretched
across the lintel above a screen door, between vertical rows
of decapitated bass and gar pikes nailed to the siding to dry
in the sun like shrunken heads.

I braked beside the van, killed the engine, got out, and
pulled my shirt away from my back, where it had stuck like
cellophane. An inland breeze cooled the sweat under my
arms, carrying a potpourri of sun-slapped water and diesel
exhaust. A Jet Ski razzed out on the lake.

Cigarette smoke nipped at my nostrils, blown out the
open window on the passenger's side of the van, where a
furniture-moving type in a black T-shirt sat resting a meaty
forearm on the ledge. WXYZ-TV covered both doors and
the front and rear fenders in letters two feet high. His
muddy brown gaze slid my way without curiosity, then returned to the screen door.

I pulled it open against the pressure of a spring and let it
shut behind me with a bang that sounded like the last day
of school. A copper bell tied to the inside handle with twine
jangled, just in case the noise couldn't be heard clear
across the lake. I waited just inside for my eyes to adjust
to the shady dim light. Steel-framed windows fronted the
water, but they were covered by bamboo shades that rolled
down from the top to cut the glare and heat.

"You shot past it," graveled a voice deep inside the gloom.

"What you want to do is turn around, go back to the main road, backtrack a mile, hang a left on Darwin, and that'll take you straight to it. Can't miss it—if you don't sneeze."

"Thanks!" A chirpy female voice; on-air talent on the hoof, with enthusiasm in case lots. I made way for a trim brunette in a silk blazer and skirt and another man built to the same scale as the one they'd left in the van, in a polo shirt and tan Dockers that hammocked his belly. They swept past me with even less interest than their companion outside, and left a mix of squash blossoms and Old Spice in their wake.

The interior of the shop looked bigger than it seemed from outside, despite a clutter of fishing rods, forty-pound bags of water softener salt in stacks, and racks of Swiss Army knives and plastic lures in blister cards hanging from hooks. The floor was built of two-foot-wide planks salvaged from some long-gone farmhouse or granary, and twelve feet of glass counter separated me from the man who'd given directions to the TV crew.

He was a thick-barreled party with white hair chopped short and stiff as wire brush, seated on a tall stool plucking at a snarl of glistening nylon line the size of a bowling ball. From that angle I couldn't see his face, but he had on a green twill worksuit with a RANDY'S MARINA patch ironed to one shirt pocket. You could buy a cap with the same patch on its crown from a bunch of them stacked like nesting dolls on the end of the counter.

"What's the story, they biting upcountry?" I asked.

"Hell." He didn't look up.

"Excuse me?"

He broke up some rocks in his throat. "Fourteen people

year round and a little pissant inn, but twice a year it's news. Halloween's the other time."

"Oh. Hell, Michigan. I didn't realize it was around here. What's the draw this season?"

" 'Just how hot is it in Hell?' This the second crew got lost looking for it this week. Channel Four beat them to it. I expect Channel Two tomorrow or the day after. That's what's happened to the news." He tore a loop free with a jerk. The line looked like piano wire and should have sliced his hand open to the bone, but the skin of his palm looked as thick as the leather patches sailors wear to stitch canvas. "I should've said three times. I forgot January."

"When it freezes over."

"Then there's April fifteenth, when folks come for the postmark on their tax returns. I guess we got us a lively little concern at that."

I grinned. "Darwin Road leads to Hell?"

He looked up then. "Think they'd get it?"

At seventy and change he was more robust-looking than Joey Ballista, but the particular shade of magenta on his bunched, razor-scraped features indicated that any of his arteries could pop any time. His circulation system was one big sheet of bubble wrap. I took out my folder and spread it on the counter. His eyes lingered on me another second, then went to the photo ID that came with the license. He ignored the honorary Wayne County sheriff's star I carried with it for the bling.

"I almost applied myself," he said, returning his attention to the tangle in his lap. "It was tough sledding those first few years. I rented five canoes total; two of 'em sunk. Local punks set fire to the place the first winter. One morning I came in and the pontoon I rented out to parties was gone. Deputies found it two days later busted up below the Delhi rapids."

"You didn't miss much. The job wouldn't keep you in fish hooks."

He wasn't finished. "Third year, this shaky bastard from Detroit put a shotgun in my back when I was out planing the dock and marched me in the back door to clean out my firearms stock. My wife was alive then, filling in at the counter. Saw us through the window, loaded a forty-four mag the way I showed her, and shot a piece out of the door frame as we were coming in. I hit the floor, as much to get out of her line of fire as because of that shotgun. He dropped it—it was a bluff, busted firing pin—and ran for the lake with Doris running after him, potting away with that big mag. When the deputies showed up he wouldn't come out of the water until they took it away from her.

"Thirty-seven years on the force, fifteen with the racket squad, I never fired my piece once outside the range. I had to retire and come out here for gunplay, what do you think of that?"

"It tells me you were a pretty good cop."

"That was the turning point. People started buying up the lakefront, knocking down the shacks and putting up houses big as airplane hangars. You got a place on the water, you need a boat and everything that comes with it. Doris got sick and died just as we were showing a profit. What's your story?"

"No retirement in sight yet." I put away the folder. "Joe Ballista."

"I heard he died."

"Me, too. He didn't get the message."

He'd stopped tugging on the line. Now he went back to it. "All the wrong people are still alive."

FIVE

His case has come up again," I said. "There's some question of his guilt."

He rotated the ball in his hands, looking for a new place to start. I didn't know whether fishing line was so expensive it was worth salvaging or he used it to keep himself busy between customers. "I asked all the questions back then. Why should the answers be different now?"

"What put you on to him?"

"We got a positive ID from the victim at the showup."

"I was there. Stackpole identified Ballista as one of the mobsters who'd threatened his life if he didn't find something else to write about. Back then he averaged two death threats a month. It didn't exactly narrow the field."

"Snitch gave him up."

"Who was the snitch?"

He leaned back, laid the snarl to rest at last on a work bench under the shaded windows, and folded his horned hands on his thick hard stomach. His eyes were pale in the deep red face with black pupils in the centers: pinhole cameras for the cop to photograph crime scenes and facial expressions. "Now, why would I give that up to you when I wouldn't for a judge?"

"The world's gone around a bunch of times. Whoever planted that dynamite, if it was Joey he's paid for it, and if it wasn't the law can't touch him. Outing the snitch won't put him in Dutch."

"Ever hear of a guy named Arnold Schuster?"

"No. Was he the snitch?"

"Not in this deal. He fingered Willie Sutton, the big-time bank robber, from a wanted poster better than fifty years ago. Schuster got his fifteen; interviews, reconstructions, all that. Albert Anastasia, the boss of Murder, Incorporated, saw him on TV and said, 'I can't stand squealers. Hit that guy!' Somebody shot Schuster down in the street a couple days later. Sutton wasn't mobbed up, Schuster was just a working stiff. There was no good reason, business or personal, to take him out. Just because the person who sent Joey over can't hurt anybody don't guarantee somebody won't hurt that person."

"When someone says 'that person,' it's usually female," I said. "Joey was married. Still is, but they've been separated a long time. Was that the reason for the break?"

He smiled. His teeth were as yellow as old plaster and ground down to stumps. "Good luck getting so much as traffic directions from a hoodlum's wife. When they marry the man they marry the outfit."

"Girlfriend, then. These guys spend as much on their mistresses as their houses, but it doesn't always take."

"I sell fishing tackle. You want to fish, rent a boat and go out on the lake. Don't light up in here," he snapped. "I fill propane tanks out back."

I left the cigarette unlit between my lips and put away the pack and matches. "Client in this case has deep pockets. You say business is good but I don't see any customers."

"It picks up in the afternoon. Weekends I hire a couple of kids to help out. But if it was a dozen years ago and I was still in hock up to my hair I'd knock you into the middle of the road over a deal like that. I'm supposed to keep my blood pressure on a leash, but I just might let it off if you don't turn around and go back to that shithole you crawled out of."

"Thanks for your time, Detective."

"I'm not a detective. When I was I didn't work for the left-handed dollar." He drew the tangle of fishing line back onto his lap.

Anyway, it had been a pretty drive.

I had lunch in Pinckney, in a country restaurant with machine-woven tapestries of deer hanging on cement-block walls and a meatloaf-and-mashed-potato combination made from the cement that was left over and nursed the beginnings of a peptic ulcer all the way back to the city. Barry's machine was still answering. I had something or nothing, but I couldn't nail down which it was without access to my personal pipeline into the rich subculture of the American Mafia. He was probably busy extending that line himself.

Well, I had another choice, but it meant crossing the DMZ between the private and public sectors, with one-way spikes in place to make the process of withdrawal a challenge.

The government in Washington needs to kick the habit of naming its buildings after real people. Half of Congress wants to chisel J. Edgar Hoover's name off FBI headquarters on account of his secret files and black-bag operations, and the federal building in downtown Detroit was christened MacNamara after a county executive who'd died while under investigation for decades of corruption. It's one of several monuments to the left-handed dollar standing inside a few square blocks, with the Coleman A. Young Municipal Center standing smack dab in the middle.

Mary Ann Thaler, U.S. Marshal, had graduated from an airless afterthought of a room intended to shelter a Xerox machine into a stuffy second-guess of an office on the next floor, where an African violet in a pot occupied the only patch of sunlight coming in through the window at an oblique angle. I found her sitting in an upholstered scoop chair reserved for visitors, with her legs crossed in silver-black hose and a file folder open on her lap.

She looked up from the steno pad on her knee when I tapped on the open door. She wore a grayish-pink linen suit that brought out the color in her complexion and gave her brown eyes a vampirish cast. She was growing her hair out against the tide of fashion, still refusing to lighten the brown to blonde, and before she swept off her reading glasses to focus on me she looked like the sexy librarian type I'd met long before the operation, when she'd still needed corrective lenses to avoid tripping over corpses in her former line of work.

"We need better security," she greeted. "Did you just come from a ball game?"

I looked down at my casual wear. "No, a lake. Deck shoes too much?"

"You almost drowned in a lake last spring, and froze to

death in another one the winter before that. I thought by now you'd enlisted for desert fighting."

"Beats sitting indoors reading. We don't get many days like this."

"Tip of the iceberg." She pointed the clicker of her ballpoint at her desk, a thundering gray steel veteran of the Rosenburg investigation, now holding up a mountainscape of thick file folders identical to the one in front of her. "When they were busy looking around for something to keep me busy, someone found boxes of records that have never been entered into the mainframe. My considerable detective experience is currently employed hunting down keywords. I'm thinking of bailing and begging for my old job back."

"Will they reinstate you as lieutenant?"

"Not in a million. I was daydreaming. The chief thinks quitting to go to work for the feds was an act of betrayal. Anyway, she's the mayor's lapdog and he never got over my turning down a spot on his security detail. He asked if I owned a bikini."

"Couldn't you have gone out and bought one?"

She didn't answer. "How much trouble are you in this time?"

"I'm thinking of bailing and begging for my old job back."

"Which was?"

"Shooting Vietcong snipers out of trees. Actually, I'm not in trouble yet, but the day's only half over. Are you still on speaking terms with the records clerks at Thirteen Hundred?"

"Every day. The department's been put in a kind of receivership, with Justice in charge. Too much coke walking out of the evidence room, you know. The brass hates the new setup, but those last-hired-first-fired types are as anxious to please as puppies. I can't lend them to you," she said.

"Why not?"

"National security."

"I'm surprised you got through that with a straight face."

"I was a little surprised myself. Personal protection, then. I'm still on probation. I haven't made it through the manual yet, but I'm pretty sure there's something in it about using a public facility for private purposes."

"I'm ahead of you on points," I said. "I hate to draw it."

"You might at least make a face or something so it looks like you do." She flipped shut the folder and crossed her legs the other way. She had long, muscular calves. I wondered if she practiced running in heels. "It hasn't been that long since you scored those points. You might think before you put them in play. I don't give them out like Hershey squares."

"They had to do with helping out John Alderdyce, a mutual friend. This favor I'm asking involves another friend. Barry Stackpole."

"But not a mutual one. I've met him twice and both times he was as cooperative as a coral reef."

"John's been the same with me since he made inspector. When I call him a friend I always expect lightning to strike me. But I tried to come through when you asked me to help him out. It almost got me blown into little pieces."

"It didn't do him any good either."

"That wasn't the deal. Anyway, that storm blew over. The police union backed down the mayor and the chief and we've still got inspectors and precincts. I need a rundown on a Combination connection."

"Combination? Oh, organized crime. That's Stackpole's beat. Ask him."

"He's unavailable. Anyway, it's about him."

"Who's the connection?"

"Joseph Michael Ballista. He's second-generation. His father bootlegged liquor when it was popular and black market goods during war rationing. Joey pioneered in smuggling Mexican Brown into Detroit."

"Before my time. I was just a margarita in my mother's glass when that was going on."

I counted back. "Didn't you and I work the Jackie Acardo murder?"

"I worked it. You were an eyewitness. It's ungentlemanly to do math in a lady's presence. What's the job?"

"I'm legging for Joey's attorney. She's working the Domino Principle on his priors, going all the way back to his first. We're reopening the case: attempted murder and aggravated assault. Maybe unlawful discharge of unlicensed fireworks inside city limits."

"Wait, dynamiting?" She had it then.

"So you do remember the case."

"The old guard doesn't clear out when the young turks join up. Listening to gossip's part of the job. Have you told Stackpole you're trying to clear the man who crippled him?"

"Allegedly trying. In case he's innocent. The field of suspects covers a lot of ground."

"So the answer's no."

"He's unavailable, I said."

She shook her head. "Ballista's not the only one around town who likes to play with explosives. You come a close second. Do you need the job so badly you'd risk screwing a friend?"

"*The* friend. Cops don't count. Someone else will take the job if I don't. He might not be as tidy with the facts. If it turns out it wasn't Joey, Barry will want to know."

"You're sure this is the thing you want to call in a solid over."

"You have to use them before the sell-by date."

She gave her head another shake, then turned the page in the pad on her knee and clicked the pen, waiting.

"I've got everything in the police files relating to the investigation," I said, "except what wasn't written down. What I need is the name of the snitch who set the dogs on Joey. The arresting officer wouldn't give it to me this morning."

"I should hope not. Every cop who ever spent a day in the tank for contempt would come back to haunt him if he did. It won't be on the record, either. That's what 'confidential informant' means."

"I had to ask anyway. It's bound to be one of Joey's known associates. I can ask Joey, but he won't be objective, and if the state of his health means anything, I don't know if I can trust his memory." I hesitated, not wanting to steer her in the wrong direction, then went ahead. "I've got a hunch it's a woman."

"Based on what?"

"The cop got cute with his pronouns. Attention to detail is good police work, but it can ball you up in casual conversation."

"Wife?"

"He as much as said no. That might've been a blind, but I doubt it. When those Mafia wives get sore they tend to take things into their own hands. I'll run it out, but I don't need your help for that. She's a Sunday supplement success story."

She made two scratches and a question mark. "What's the cop's name? If Ms. X was his snitch and she had a sheet, he might show up on it as arresting officer. That'd narrow the search."

"Randolph Severin. He retired to the life aquatic at a place called Portage Lake, out by Hell."

"That explains your morning. I think I remember the name. He was going out as I was coming in. Tough rep."

"Not as tough as Mrs. Severin. She almost blew his head off one time saving him from bad guys."

"Sure it was the bad guys she was shooting at?" She wrote some more, reminders to herself for her eyes only. "Go through Hell while you were there?"

"No more than usual."

"You will."

SIX

My office smelled like an old leather trunk that had been shut up for months. I tossed the arrest file I'd gotten from Lucille Lettermore onto the desk, opened the window, and switched on the oscillating fan, making a brief angry vortex in the dust that rose from the blotter. Another followed the first when I sat down and plunked the Yellow Pages on top of the file.

In the Interior Decorators and Designers section, a photo of a living room in military order invited me in from the borders of a quarter-page ad.

CAN'T SEE FOR CLUTTER?
LET "I" CARE IMPROVE YOUR VISION
IONA'S SIMPLE SOLUTIONS
Iona Cuneo, Chief Designer
407 Ottawa St., Iroquois Heights

Iona Ballista, née Cuneo, was a local success story with an international impact, if you counted the work she'd done on the official quarters of a Canadian prime minister, who'd been roundly criticized in Parliament for taking his business across the border; the fact that she was married to a known U.S. racketeer was scarcely mentioned. After obtaining a legal separation from her husband, she'd invested the money awarded her for living expenses, first in a course on interior decorating, then in a small suite of offices in Redford Township that became a large suite in Iroquois Heights once her spare approach to furnishing and ornament caught on in the suburbs. The excess of the Reagan years had played its part. She'd gotten a jump start, some said, when marriage to a chronic defendant living among the multicultural bric-a-brac amassed by a father-in-law with no taste for collecting proved suffocating; friends had complimented her on the simple elegance of her apartment in Redford and encouraged her to go professional. A tasteful advertising campaign and word-of-mouth from satisfied customers had led to the Canadian gig, and she'd parlayed that political controversy into a PR blitz free of charge courtesy of the media.

At the height of the flap she'd granted an interview to a reporter doing a cover story for the combined *Detroit News* and *Free Press* Sunday magazine, then sued when the headline christened her "The Moll of Mode." More than ever she'd become interested in putting past associations behind her.

I thought that was a good place to start.

The Brit receptionist I got on the line cross-examined me for thirty seconds, established I wasn't a preferred client or ever likely to be, and was about to hang up when I said, "Tell her it's about Joey Ballistic."

A full second slid down the wire. "I have instructions not to put through anyone using that name. I'm sorry."

I got the dial tone and called back.

"Me again," I said, before she could rattle off the name of the store. "It's either me or the cops, and they're less Zen-like about getting hung up on. Joey's red hot again."

This time I listened to part of a rap cover of "Lush Life." Miss Savile Row came back on. "Would you repeat the name, please?"

"Joey Ballistic. B as in Burglar. A as in Alibi. L as in—"

"Not that one. Your name."

I told her. I'd forgotten what *L* stood for anyway. She went away again. I heard a few more bars, if that's what they come in, and put down the receiver to light a cigarette. I could feel the bass pulsing in the soles of my feet. The receptionist was saying "Hello?" for the second time when I picked up.

"Does that really bring in business?" I asked. "Don't hip-hop fans usually decorate with milk crates and bullet holes?"

"Iona has an on-site consultation, but she'll be in the office this evening. Seven o'clock?"

So it was Iona. Few tyrants can compare with those who run their businesses like a democracy.

I had four hours. I used part of them to go through the police file and the report by Reliance Investigations. The onionskin the department used back then was as thin as moth's wings; you had to separate the sheets with a fingernail and spread them out to keep from reading page 3 along with page 1. I had to hold some of them up to the light in order to read the typing, which had been done on old ribbons to begin with and hadn't become any more legible with age. Glop had made black circles of lowercase *o*'s and *e*'s, and the combination of fragile paper and fingers best designed for spearing doughnuts had made more holes than a piano roll. Rotting Building Syndrome had allowed the urban elements to weep all over the forensics report, smearing bureaucratic verbiage and crucial information indiscriminately. Official neglect is worse than a coverup; when you've traced neglect to its source, all you're left with is an estimate for repairs.

The investigation Lucille Lettermore had paid for wasn't much more enlightening. Ernest Krell, the CEO—in semi-retirement now, which meant he didn't put in any more than sixty hours a week at the office—had been in military intelligence, and the kind of experience-fueled speculation that breaks cases more often than not was prohibited from the written record. I found out that Detective First Grade Randolph Severin, retired, was still available for questioning in regard to the Ballista arrest, and the hours his marina was open for business, items I'd already gotten from Lucille and the Livingston County Yellow Pages. The rest was rehash. No wonder she'd called me. I couldn't match Reliance for collective skill or equipment, but I didn't charge for information she could have gotten in the microfilm reading room at the Detroit Public Library for free.

What I'd have liked more than anything was an hour or so over drinks with someone who could report in detail what went on during bull sessions in Krell's office; but breach of confidence was a capital crime at Reliance so far as a professional investigator's career was concerned. He paid for the conceit: His collection of crack detectives lured from the public to the private sectors was the largest in North America. I'd resisted two or three attempts to recruit me on grounds of the currency value of information shared for information gained, as well as of the impossibility of working for someone like Krell, who kept a personally autographed photo of G. Gordon Liddy on the wall behind his desk next to his honorable discharge.

But then, nothing anyone else can tell you goes as far toward closing an investigation as the stuff you go out and bring back yourself, with the personal investment of mortal peril or just common everyday abuse. I had the scars to prove it, and $1,157.56 in cold hard cash in the bank.

I'd been to Iroquois Heights many times. Most of them I'd come away from without having been shot, shot at, hit in the head, or arrested; but once is all you need to pause on the way for personal protection. It had been less than ten but more than once. I clipped the Chief's Special to my belt in the spot where it had worn a hollow in my right kidney and pointed the Cutlass north.

A feral growth of civic-center buildings sprouted beyond flat tracks of suburban housing, with the ruins of the old Stutch Motors plant still awaiting demolition atop its gaunt hill. I slowed to negotiate a zigzag main drag around trees in boxes and gooseneck lamps, new since a fleet of trucks had destroyed the plant and much of downtown, a man-made disaster I'd had a hand in. The construction had gone far enough over budget to draw fire from state and federal watchdogs, so the work had shut down after three blocks and detours put in place to direct traffic around raw earth where pavement had been stripped away. A deli and a gift shop had already closed up in the inaccessible block. The city was going through one of those periodic recessions that eat it from the inside, but the people in office never seemed to notice.

Iona's Simple Solutions appeared to be surviving in style. It occupied the ground floor front of a renovated hardware store in a block the city hadn't monkeyed with yet, with a stucco façade and the name of the design firm in cursive on a sign shaped like a lily pad. People were home eating supper, and I had no trouble finding parking in front. It cost me a quarter more per hour than it had the last time I'd been in town. Cities all over the country are ripping out their meters to encourage business away from the malls. Not there.

I passed through an air lock into a peach-colored reception room with a C-shaped desk and architects' drawings in frames. The English voice on the telephone belonged to a woman sitting inside the curve of the *C*, slitting envelopes with one of those knives that stick out of country squires' backs in British murder mysteries. I hadn't expected Dame Agnes Twilly, but something in tweed with a face that looked as if it would gobble apples from your hand. I got ash blonde hair, high cheeks with color in them, lips that curved up slightly, anticipating some kind of punchline, squarish shoulders and a good collarbone in a blouse with a soft blue sheen and a spread collar. "Mr. Walker, is it?" She looked up from under long lashes by the only light burning in the room, a banker's lamp on the desk with a green glass shade. "Iona's waiting for you in the model room."

Her directions took me down an L-shaped hallway past pictures I couldn't see because the ceiling lights were shut off, at the end of which stood a door that belonged on the front of a house. A mullioned window with opaque panes let light out. When an invitation followed my knock I almost wiped my feet on the carpet before turning the knob.

"I can't give you much time. I'm flying to China in the morning to confer with a client and I don't sleep well on planes."

Iona Cuneo Ballista had taken better care of her body than her husband had of his. She sat on a sofa made of clear plastic tubing and white terry with her feet tucked under her, playing solitaire with color samples on a table made of bent sheet metal that stayed up in that same mysterious way that let women keep their shoes on without slings or straps. She wore tailored slacks and a sleeveless blouse and wore her hair, black with red highlights, in a modified 60s beehive slanting over one eye, no bra nor much need for one, but I'm not much of a mammary man. She was ten years younger than Joey and looked ten years younger than that, a slim woman who appeared taller sitting down than she would standing up.

The room looked like someone was about to move out or getting ready to move in: a pair of chairs that matched the sofa, bare walls, no lamps or vases, painted and carpeted two shades of gray, lit from behind soffits. "What is it with you Ballistas and empty space?" I asked.

"I heard Joey cleared out a bunch of crap. If he did that when I was around, I'd still be around. I could *live* with Joey. I could *live* with the crap. I couldn't live with both."

Thirty years in Michigan hadn't taken much of the Brooklyn brass out of her tone. The story was she'd met both Joes during a father-son trip east to hammer out a free-trade agreement between the Detroit underworld and the dons of the five New York boroughs. Her father was one of the dons and she'd performed hostess duty in lieu of a late mother. The marriage had started Senior and Junior's climb from spear carriers to capos.

"This where you take customers so they know what they're in for? What kind of person wants to live in an airport waiting room?"

"The kind of person who doesn't want to live in a museum in the Bloomies. They call ours a throwaway society, only nobody ever throws anything away. Cluttered house, cluttered mind. Broken-field thinking, I call it. One of the main reasons the Bourbon kings failed to observe a revolution brewing against them is they were preoccupied with their upholstered furniture and mathematically correct gardens. A mind can't breathe without space for oxygen to circulate."

"Feng shui."

"Feng shui," she corrected; although I failed to hear any difference in pronunciation. "I never use that term. It's New Wave, and there's nothing more old-fashioned than that." She made a sweeping gesture with an arm and hand unencumbered by rings, bracelets, and French manicuring. "This is basically an empty canvas. I bring them in here, let them walk around, furnish and decorate the place in their head. Adding's easier than subtracting."

"Too right-brain for me. I flunked algebra. So did Einstein."

She gave me the Eye. The other was screened behind her coiffure. I'd seen someone like her in a forty-year-old movie, singing "Domani" during an expository scene. I'd forgotten the exposition, but remembered the singer. "Why should I explain?" she said. "You're not here to hire me, and if you were you wouldn't be here. Minimalists don't wear neckties."

I'd stopped at home to change back into the suit; a mistake, I knew now. Even so there were a couple of things wrong with that sentence, but I wasn't there to correct her usage either. I gave her a card.

She shuffled her samples into a deck and slid it aside to read. "You need heavier stock, and sans-serif letters. It looks like a funeral announcement." She held it out.

"Keep it. I'm having them printed more than one at a time now. They get shopworn after ten or twelve times."

"Really, take it back. I'd just throw it away. I avoid accumulating things, and I've gotten this far without having to hire an investigator."

I returned it to my wallet. "That old bombing case of Joey's is back on the front burner. His attorney thinks she can have it set aside."

"Why? He paid that bill years ago."

"It's complicated. I don't understand it myself, but that's the job."

"I wouldn't know anything that would help. I'm a Mafia brat, you know. They don't confide in their wives or sweethearts."

"You must have overheard a thing or two over the years. The house isn't that big. I was there yesterday." It seemed longer.

"The place was a lot smaller, with all that crap. I made a number of concessions in return for my independence. Our church doesn't recognize divorce, but it frowns nearly as heavily on legal separation. I think the legal part is what made Joey and his associates nervous. I don't discuss our marriage with strangers. The penalties are substantial."

I thought about the cash in my wallet. It wouldn't make a dimple in her rent. "If that's true, I'm wasting your time and his. The investigation seems to have swung on an inside informant."

"If I was a snitch, he'd be a widower. If you'd told Marcine that was what you were after, I could have told you the same thing over the phone."

"Marcine, that's her name? It sounds like a cologne."

"I don't hire them for their names. Her accent's worth three hundred thousand in advertising, but I don't hire them for that either. How old would you guess she is?"

"She could coast along at thirty."

"She's forty-six. Experience is the coin. I wish you'd told her. I could have saved you a trip."

"Telephones aren't for identifying snitches."

"Well, you have your answer." She cut a sample from the middle of the deck like a sharp and recorded the order number on the back in a Post-it pad two inches square using a flat pen no longer than her thumb. I figured she used an envelope for a handbag.

"Not the one I came for. Tell me about the sweetheart."

SEVEN

She hoisted her one visible eyebrow, an inverted comma plucked a hair short of excessive. A slide rule would have been a sex toy for her. "I said wives *or* sweethearts, not *and*. It's an insult to a woman to suggest she couldn't satisfy her man."

"At five hundred a day, my clients can't afford the time it takes to be diplomatic. Anyway, it's a question of form, not satisfaction. In Joey's set, a mistress is like a fax machine. If you don't have one, you're too far outside the loop to do business with. Sam Lucy went to his reward a hundred thousand in the hole on bridge points to his bimbo. I doubt they'd been to bed in years."

"Sam couldn't play cards for shit. She was the only one who didn't let him win. *Bimbo*'s harsh. You have no idea what kind of time investment is involved in maintaining a man's interest against constant competition. It's actually a relief to find out he isn't out topping the barnyard. Having a mistress is the new monogamy."

"Old's the new new, yellow's the new puce, Putin's the new

Mary-Kate Olsen. People don't listen to themselves or they'd say something that makes sense. What was her name?"

"I didn't say there was a name."

I wanted to smoke, but I didn't bother looking for an ashtray to find out if it was okay. A single nicotine stain would have thrown the entire room out of balance. I stuck my hands in my pockets. "I can't offer money. You're sitting on my net worth, and it's too early in the job to go back to the well as deep as I'd have to go to get you to look at me instead of swatches. I think the reason Joey unloaded his tchotchkes is he's broke. If he goes back inside, his legal expenses will eat the house and whatever else the paper chase turns up. Outside, he has a chance to work something with his old contacts. But then I don't suppose whatever he's paying you for all those wasted years would be missed. You've got Canadian premieres and Chinese industrialists on the hook."

"He's in shipping, and I think you're well aware that any growing concern has to keep investing the same money over and over until the first investment shows black. When the dice stops rolling, you're finished. I need that allowance to live on while all my working capital is tied up. But if you're trying to scare me into ratting out a rat, you'd better do better than you're doing."

She untucked her feet, long and narrow for her height but well tended in plain linen slippers. "I've seen Joey when he had to carry his keys in his hand because his pockets were stuffed with cash, and I've seen him when he didn't have a quarter to tip the kid who brought him his *Racing Form*, but there was never a time when he couldn't raise case dough on his reputation alone. His poor choices put him in jail, but his good ones always made money for him and his partners.

Two things Sicilians never forget are money and insults, and they'll forget an insult if you give them enough money."

"He tips quarters? Maybe it was the *Racing Form* kid who rolled over on him."

"You don't think that. You've got it in your head it was a woman. Why, because we can't keep our mouths shut?"

"You spent the last five minutes proving that wrong. It's just a hunch I have. What about the mistress?"

"No kidding, Joey's busted?"

"His investment situation was a lot like yours. It worked as long as the lawyers he paid to keep him out of a cell block earned their keep, but when Congress tied a knot in the Bill of Rights, he blew his living expenses and his working capital filing for appeals that got turned back when they reached Washington. After that it was like feeding coins into a slot machine that never paid out."

"I'm first in line for the house if he defaults on my claim."

"Detroit's crawling with customers looking for six thousand square feet in property taxes. You'll probably find a buyer about the time you grow your second appendix."

"You seem pretty sure I can get him out of the hole."

"This time he's got Lucille Lettermore."

The eyebrow arched again. "I've heard of her. He hired a woman lawyer?"

"Yeah, and the others were doing so well."

"She gets terrorism suspects out of Guantanamo. Nobody gets terrorism suspects out of Guantanamo."

"Gangsters are small change after that. If she can Pluto that first conviction, everything else goes away."

"And all I have to do to have Joey to draw on like a bank is give up his girlfriend."

"Win-win," I said.

"What if she isn't the snitch?"

"I cross her name off the list and move on. Progress."

She slid a finger along the crooked veil of hair that covered one eye. "Can I interest you in a job selling interior design?"

"My heart wouldn't be in it. I'm a broken-field thinker by trade."

"Too bad. I can use a man in sales who doesn't wear tangarine-colored slippers. The stereotypes will strangle you in this business."

"Mine too. I don't own a trenchcoat."

"Would you ask Marcine to come in here, please?"

"You won't lock me out if I do?"

"If I wanted to get rid of you I'd have you thrown out. I didn't give up all my husband's friends when I gave up my husband."

I left her and went to the end of the hall. The woman at the desk let me wait while she slit five more pieces of mail. When she looked up I said, "She wants you."

She put down the stiletto and rose, smoothing her skirt. She still looked thirty, but I should have seen the extra mileage in the way she handled herself. I'd expected her to pick up a steno pad or something, but she entered the hall empty-handed on four-inch heels. She was runway tall even without them, and there was still something of the strut in the way she worked her hips and ankles. I followed, admiring. I had to hustle to get ahead of her to open the door. She wasn't the kind that waited.

When we entered, employer and employee exchanged a look. Marcine walked across and folded herself into a tube-

and-terry chair, crossing one long leg over the other and looking up at me from under the silver-blonde hair, which slanted across her forehead in the opposite direction of Iona's, without covering an eye. Disregarding that and the height difference, they might have been negatives of each other.

A second passed in silence.

"Oh," I said then. I can take a hint when it kicks me on the chin.

EIGHT

I was a Jaguar spokesmodel when I met Joe," Marcine said. She said *jag-yoo-ar*; the English won't pronounce a foreign name properly even if it means another shot at empire. "I found out later the reason most wiseguys visit the auto show is to troll for models. I stood on a revolving stand next to an XKE—sapphire blue, fourteen coats of paint, deep as Lake Superior. I was sixteen years old, wearing a white evening gown worth as much as my father made in a year, rattling off the top speed, compression ratio, and cylinder displacement of a car that cost more than the house I grew up in. I still remember my spiel, if you care to hear it."

"Maybe over drinks." I was seated in a matching chair, which was surprisingly comfortable once I got over the fear that it would fold up under my weight. "So do you communicate with eyelashes, or did you talk all this over before I got here?"

Iona said, "Neither. Ours is an unusual situation. It may even be unique. When my father put away his disappointment that I was born without a penis, he bought me the best education he could by endowing buildings, but I can't think of anything in history or literature to compare with a cuckolded wife offering her rival a job. Not on the up-and-up, at any rate, without a scheme to sneak cyanide into her coffee."

"Tea." The other wrinkled her nose briefly. "My parents brought me to this country when I was twelve and I've yet to assimilate to the shock of all that caffeine. It's no wonder you're the leaders of the free world. You never sleep."

"Don't you love hearing her talk? I take her on buying trips to London just to brush up on her accent. Anyway, a situation like ours is bound to come up in conversation sooner or later. Keeping a woman on the side is an impossible secret to maintain. Too many people are in on it: Landlords, apartment-house managers, dressmakers, package liquor stores, not to mention your friends, who are the real reason you men step out in the first place; otherwise it's like buying one of Marcine's Jag-yoo-ars and never taking it out of the garage. The relationship will arouse curiosity. Who said the only way to avoid curiosity is to satisfy it?"

"Nobody," I said. "Oscar Wilde said the only way to avoid temptation is to succumb to it."

"Oh, dear. I've spent too much time with stylebooks lately and not enough with the classics. But you take my point." She turned to Marcine. "Mr. Walker wants to know who dropped the dime on Joey in that attempted murder case."

" 'Dropped the dime?' Oh, yes; the American idiom. Every time I think I understand it, it changes. I've also lost track of *which* attempted murder case. For a while there it seemed like someone was always serving him a warrant for something. I'm afraid I was frightfully stupid then. Perhaps that was part of my charm."

I fiddled with the crease in my trousers. I was just getting used to having one. " 'Frightfully.' Wot ho, and all that rot. You spread it thick."

"I know that one. Yes, I suppose I do that. Iona encourages me. Americans want their mechanics to be German, their hairdressers homosexual, and their receptionists English, if they can get them. I've never been to Wimbledon, and the only place I've seen the Queen is on the telly, but that would only drive away clients. So, yes, I spread it thick." Suddenly her face went slack and her mouth turned ugly. "Wha' a soight, lydie; pull the shydes or tyke in 'arf a bob for the show." She beamed, refinement restored. "What if I were to answer the telephone like that? I should have said that Americans prefer their English from the West End."

Iona laughed, not without an edge. It had sounded like genuine Whitechapel cockney, which to her must have been like finding a muddy galosh on a white-on-white carpet. "She has a great ear, doesn't she? It was her sense of humor and irony that made me decide to hire her. I knew all about her history with Joey, but that hadn't anything to do with why I left. I needed someone at the front desk, I liked her, and she was okay with the salary I could afford. That was many raises ago."

"Did you turn Joey?" I asked Marcine.

"Turn him?"

"Peach on him. Give him up to the traps. Top him for the peelers. Tell a cop it was Joey who tried to blow a newspaper reporter to pieces with a fistful of dynamite."

"Oh. *That* attempted murder. No. Is that what this is

about? No. I was dreadfully angry when he threw me over for a younger woman—I was almost eighteen—and I won't say I wouldn't have betrayed him if I had that information, but he never discussed his business in my company. If someone came to the apartment he always went for a walk with whoever it was, leaving me inside. In two years I never saw him answer the telephone, and the few times I did when it was for him, he refused to take it. I'm sorry I can't be more help, but to be frank, he only trusted me in what you Yanks call the sack."

"I'll vouch for that. My father made the mistake of discussing an item of business over a tapped wire. They only let him out of prison to die. Joey never forgot that. All the time I lived with him he only used the telephone to get the odds from Atlantic City. It was an incredible luxury, when I moved out, to be able to order a pizza from my living room."

"This doesn't sound like a man who'd take the risk of hands-on murder," I said.

Iona said, "Joey's blue-collar. He got restless sitting behind a desk. He'd come home sometimes sweating like a Teamster. Some nights he didn't come home at all, but when he spent them with Marcine or one of the others he always showered. When he stunk I knew he'd been doing gruntwork of some kind. He couldn't stay away from the nuts and bolts."

"How many others were there?"

Iona shook her head. Marcine shrugged, smiling. "What about the younger girl he dumped you for?" I asked Marcine.

"I never saw her or heard her name. We were having a

fight and he threw her age up to me, trying to make me seem like some old hag. I threw a lamp at him."

"Dangerous projectile," Iona said. "I avoid them in my designs."

"Any idea who did roll over on him?" I looked from one to the other. Iona shook her head again. Marcine shrugged, smiling.

I looked at my watch, although I didn't care what time it was. I thanked them and stood.

"Sorry you wasted your evening," Iona said.

"It's not like Detroit has a nightlife."

But the evening hadn't been wasted. It's easier to tell when you're being lied to face-to-face.

I got home at ten o'clock with my drive-in burger lying on the bottom of my stomach like a pirate ship in a goldfish bowl, dumped a glass of Scotch on top of it to break it up, poured another, and sipped it in my armchair while I waited for Lucille to pick up in her office. Home for her was only a place to close her eyes.

"I told you to report when you had something," she said when I finished talking. "You don't have to prove you're working. I'm buying results, not reassurances."

"It's not as bad as that. I got more out of Severin than I expected; he's a little rusty. Iona and Marcine double-teamed me. I found that significant."

"It sure was. You stumbled into a trap set by amateurs."

"Don't knock amateurs. Billie Jean King was an amateur. Mafia women are accustomed to being grilled because of their associations, so they maneuvered me out of splitting them up so I could compare their stories afterwards and bob for discrepancies. Why would they bother to do that if they had nothing to hide?"

"No one has nothing to hide. George Carlin said there are no innocent bystanders. Maybe they're overcharging their clients for furniture and chintz."

"At the risk of going up against the wisdom of a lounge comic, I have to say the manufacturers are already over-charging for the furniture Iona uses, and she wouldn't touch a yard of chintz with a pair of fire tongs. They both know I'm not with the Better Business Bureau."

"They'd feel safer if you were. The BBB's got fewer teeth than the Red Wings. But I see where you're going—although calling Carlin a lounge comic is hitting below the belt. Which one do you think's the snitch?"

"I need to hear from Mary Ann Thaler before I commit, but based on what I have I'd guess Marcine, unless she lied about being bitter when Joey cut her loose. Iona's a dark horse at best. No one goes as far as she has without know-ing she had something on the ball to start. She had no rea-son to cling to Joey, so the spurned-woman angle doesn't scan."

"So what's your strategy?"

"Divide and conquer. Tail Marcine until she slips up. If she turned on Joey, she'll turn on Joey's ex, and I can use that to drive a wedge between them. It's going to cost your client in hours. She's on her guard now, and if she's as clever as I know she is, she'll hunker in until she's sure I've given up."

"You think it'll play out that way?"

"I wouldn't bet on it. No battle plan ever survives the first encounter with the enemy."

"Who said that?"

"I think it was Custer. This is a bull session, Lucille. Come up with something better and I'll lay the bricks."

Clocks ticked on her end. I'd have laid even money she amplified the sound for the benefit of telephone consultations.

"Money's no problem," she said finally. "I can carry Joey's IOU until he's back on his feet and dealing, but if the A.G. decides to steam ahead on the uttering-and-publishing charge, I won't be able to concentrate the attention I need to make that dynamiting conviction fade away. Can you force the issue without it coming back and biting us on the ass?"

"Have you seen my ass?"

"I could nail you for sexual harassment on that statement alone, but what would I get?"

"My record collection. Turntable too, but it's been busted since Bush Forty-one."

She set that aside in the interest of time. "I'll rephrase. Can you force the issue?"

"Sure. I can't guarantee a couple of statutes won't get bent out of shape in the process."

"The law's like Gumby. You can always bend it back the way it was. Shit. Are you talking to me on a landline?"

"Yes. Didn't it come up on your ID?"

"Don't have one. You need a court order to get the records from the phone company, but any dick with a wandering thumb can access ID."

"How do you screen out telemarketers?"

"They chiseled me in stone on the Do Not Call list after I fought Ma Bell to a bloody draw. I never discuss legal details on a cell, but for whoever's listening anyway, that was a joke about bending the law. I'm an officer of the court, sworn to uphold the U.S. Constitution and the standard of ethics endorsed by the American Bar Association, spineless fudge-packers that they are. Do what you need to do, and don't call me till it's done."

I held on to the receiver until a disembodied voice advised me to hang up and dial again, then cradled the instrument. When the Reaper came for Lucille Lettermore, he'd better bring the sheriff and a waiver protecting him from legal action.

The ice in my drink looked like weak dumplings floating in watery grease. I thought about rebuilding it from scratch, but suddenly my body went as slack as Marcine's face when she did her Eliza Doolittle impression; that was what had set my suspicions on edge. Anyone who could shift character like gears put me on the balls of my feet. I threw in a couple of cubes, poured in just enough to float them, drank it off in three long drafts, and rode the buzz to bed.

It was a bad plan, or maybe a good one given the circumstances. One drink past the limit puts you to sleep; a half drink more brings you wide awake in the middle of black oblivion, like a downstroke on an electric guitar. I was alert as I've ever been when the hammering came to my door.

On the way I scooped up the Chief's Special. For the first time in memory I didn't lay it aside when the face in the peephole turned out to belong to Barry Stackpole.

NINE

hadn't seen Barry drunk in years. He could pound down whiskey sours by the hour without slurring a syllable, and the few times I'd seen him bent under a load he'd managed to pass out without offending his host, hop up the next morning, and write Pulitzer prose over a breakfast beer. When drinking companions who didn't know him well asked if he had a hollow leg, he raised the artificial one and knocked on it.

The man on my doorstep wasn't that Barry. His eyes were swimming in blood, his fair hair stuck up where the steel plate plugged his skull, and he stumbled without moving his feet. He could still pass for a college kid, but only if his frat was located in Darfur. Tidy by nature, he had half his shirt hanging outside his waistband and grass stains on the knees of his slacks. He smelled like a four-truck pileup at Jim Beam.

"So sorry for the hour," he said, almost too steadily. He was on his guard. "You look cute in a bathrobe."

"You look like a chemical spill. This a party or a wake?

Distillery's the business to get into. The customers come in either way."

"So clever, so late. You've been out, I guess. I tried to call you several times."

"I work some nights." I moved aside. He high-stepped over the low threshold, tripped on a shadow on the floor, but caught himself. "Bar still open?"

"We never close. How about a pot of coffee as an aperitif?"

"With toast and jam, when the sun's up. I'm partial to Scotch this season, but in a pinch I can make do with Janitor in a Drum."

"I've got a bottle that goes both ways." There's no use trying to sober up a determined sot. Their red cells gang up to resist it.

He made it to the armchair and lowered himself into it as carefully as if it were a tub of scalding water. He limped only slightly when all his brain cells were sparking, not at all when he was sloshed. You never knew he came without all his original parts until he made a joke about it. He was still awake when I came back from the kitchen with a couple of glasses heavy on ice. He scowled at his. "Looks like *The March of the Penguins*. What are you doing, defrosting your refrigerator?"

"Drink it up and I'll take it easy next time. In this heat I like to suck on the cubes." I took mine over to the spavined sofa and found a space between the springs I could live with. I'd picked it out with a wife I hadn't thought about in months.

He slurped, made a face. "Scotch, I said. Squeezing it out of a bagpipe doesn't count."

"It came in a big plastic jug, with a toy. It hasn't been a Glenlivet kind of year."

"I hear it's looking up."

I set aside my glass. "Dump it out, Barry. It's too late in the shift for nuance and innuendo."

He shook his head and took another pull. They say it's possible to drink yourself sober, but he was still in search of the formula. "I'm just in from Montreal. It's just as hot there. You need to go as far as Newfoundland for relief."

"Why didn't you?"

"It wasn't a pleasure trip. French-Canadian mug who used to pal around with Carlo Marcello in New Orleans was making nice with al Qaeda over importing undesirables into North America. Turns out he was kidding, but an Islamist with a sense of humor is like a feminist who doesn't look like Casey Stengel. They sent his head by special messenger to Mountie headquarters in Ottawa."

"What'd they do with the rest of him?"

"That never turns up, and no one ever seems to ask. Heads are prime rib on the hostage market."

"Well, at least you got to brush up on your French."

"Not much. It's more like border-town Spanish up there. What are *you* working on?"

"I tried to call you about it. I didn't know you were out of town."

"I bet you tried. Three people who'd been trying to reach me called one after the other five minutes after I got in the door. They all had the same message." He put down the rest of his drink and stuck out the glass. "This time neat."

I dumped out the ice in the sink, poured in three fingers, and brought it back to him. I remained standing. "I called in a marker from Mary Ann Thaler when I couldn't reach you," I said. "She got right on it, I guess. I don't imagine she was one of the ones who called you."

"She didn't have to. I've been priming the pump at Thirteen Hundred for years. She's been asking around about Joseph Michael Ballista's known associates. Ordinarily I wouldn't think much about it, but she's no longer with the DPD, and she's only interested in the circles he swam around in almost thirty years ago. That was just about the time I was learning to walk on timber."

"Was it really wooden back then?"

"It was polystyrene, same as now, but when I drink I get poetic. You're pretty tight with Thaler."

"I ain't either. Just a known associate."

"Who's the client?"

"Lucille Lettermore."

"I know Lefty Lucy. Ted Kaczynski had her number in his Rolodex. When did she become a mob mouthpiece?"

"When the Justice Department took over the rackets. She's reopening your case."

"It was never closed. We never found out if Joey was working for himself or someone else. He didn't give up a name."

"Cold, then. She wants to wipe it off his record along with some others so he can walk on his latest beef as a first-time offender."

He took a stiff gulp, shuddered when it mixed with whatever he'd started on. "You the only sleuth in town didn't fly north for the summer?"

"I inherited the job from Reliance. It's piecework, not general assembly. Lucille isn't just grandstanding. She's convinced it was a bum rap."

"That's her story. What's yours?"

"Maybe Joey didn't give up any names because he didn't have any to give."

"I hear he's in a bad way," he said after a moment. "You see a sick man, you forget what he was like when he wasn't sick. That's how parole boards get fooled."

"I was standing as close to him as I am to you when he said he never killed a man he wasn't looking in the eye."

"He didn't kill me."

"You know what he meant."

"I knew what he meant when he told me to my face I was dead but still breathing, and I knew what he meant when I hit the ground just ahead of the rest of me not twenty-four hours later. Ten fingers are only important to watchmakers and pianists, and I've just about forgotten what it was like to get out of bed without reaching for my leg ahead of my pants, but I get headaches you could boil borscht on. It's like my brain's chewing tinfoil. I know what he meant when I'm screaming for the pain to stop."

"Barry, I've spent almost as much time with these sons of bitches as you. I know when they're putting me on. Then there's Joey's record; not his sheet downtown, I mean the stuff that didn't stick because the evidence was thin. When he used a gun he stood close enough to leave powder burns on his man. He took a couple of turns with a knife and one with a garrote, probably for sentimental reasons. Right up until he got too high on the ladder to do his own hits, he never once used so much as a rifle, or anything else that wouldn't put him face to face with the vic. The lawyer who lost that case couldn't very well use that in his defense, but it says plenty to me. Smart crooks don't change their lay."

"Who ever said Joey Ballistic was smart?"

"Smart enough not to go down on any of the lifer plays."

"Smarter, maybe. He used a new MO to throw the cops off track."

"That's dumb smart. It only works in movies, and if he thought it worked at all he wouldn't have tipped his hand by threatening you in the first place. What'd you do to set him off, by the way?"

"I don't remember. As to your point, half a dozen sticks of dynamite can usually be counted on to prevent a positive ID from the victim at the showup."

"We could shuffle this deck all day. Try this angle: If Joey didn't do it, whoever did got away clean."

"What if he did? He cheated the statute of limitations when he screwed up. The clock never runs out on murder, but there's a sell-by date on attempted. That expired more than twenty years ago."

I said, "Argue all you want. It won't convince me you don't care if the wrong man pays the bill for all that aspirin you eat. You and Lucille have a couple of things in common. One is you both put plenty of store in small-*j* justice."

"So let him rot for what he got away with."

"Try it again. You didn't sell it the first time."

He gathered his feet close to the base of the chair; the thigh muscle he used to bring the artificial leg into line stood out like steel cable. The glass creaked in his fist. The laws of equal pressure were against his crushing it, but he'd been known to break a law or two in the interest of the greater good.

I pushed it; I was curious. "I need you on this, Barry.

Mary Ann's good, but disinterested. The system's not proof against an honest-to-Christ vigilante on a crusade."

The science question went unanswered for the time being. He turned on his pelvis, placed the glass on the telephone stand at his elbow with delicate precision, and came back around in one smooth movement with all the torque required to launch himself from the chair and swing a long beautiful left hook that caught me on the corner of the jaw and put me out to the count of thirty.

I'm a connoisseur of unconsciousness. You're seldom all the way out on the instant. Just before I slipped under I heard him quite clearly: "We're done, you keyhole-peeking bastard. Dead and buried. I don't see you on the street, I don't hear you on the phone. You're a ghost."

TEN

I t wasn't the first time I'd come to myself with nothing but a scrap of rug between my back and the floor; I'm a charter member of that club. But it was a first for *my* floor, not counting the couple of times I hadn't made it from bottle to bed. That made it convenient to the bathroom. I took care of the nausea that always follows like a beer chaser and ran cold water on a washcloth to poke at my jaw. I had a lump there the size of a damaging hailstone and a corker of a plum-colored bruise, but my molars were sound. Barry's light leg kept him from bracing himself for a true Tommy Hearns.

I found a dented sofa cushion on the floor where he'd slid it under my head before he left. That was something to build on in case I missed the friendship. Just then the possibility seemed remote.

The ice in my drink had melted a little, not enough to indicate I'd been out more than a few minutes. I tried medicating the bruise from the inside, but the stuff tasted like Mercurochrome. It really had been squeezed from a bagpipe.

I dumped it and what was left of Barry's drink in the kitchen sink, swallowed four aspirins, and turned in. The throbbing kept me awake for an hour, but the long, long day won out at the finish.

I came back around in sunlight with my head tucked under one wing like a cormorant. A pulsing pain bounced like a tennis ball between my sore jaw and my stiff neck. My tongue felt like rock wool. I'd had worse mornings. I got up and drank glass after glass of water, then scrambled eggs and chewed them on one side. I found relief from the dull ache in the roots of my teeth by letting hot black coffee pool for a couple of seconds there before swallowing. I'd definitely had worse mornings.

Someone who sounded like he was trying very hard not to sound like Chuck Norris answered at the federal building when I dialed the number from my uneasy chair back at ringside. He handed me off to a woman who peeled the foil off Mary Ann Thaler's name, then let me sit in on part of a Toby Keith concert before the line clicked and Thaler came on. "Want to surprise anyone who calls?" I said when she knew who I was. "Put on Dixie Chicks."

"I'll suggest that, right after I give notice. What sort of phone are you using? You sound like you're talking through a mattress."

"I stopped a line drive with my chin. Did you know the DPD's full of leaks?"

"Why should it be any different from the roof? I've got a list-a Ballista buddies from the time period you want. It reads like the Palermo phone book, but there aren't many women on it. I don't suppose you have a fax machine yet."

"I can't afford to feed one. Is there a Marcine on it?"

"Marcine Marie Logan, U.K., naturalized U.S. citizen, age eighteen at the time of the report, known to subject socially. Why'd I stick my neck out if you already have this stuff?"

"I don't. I'm working the same neighborhood only in a different decade. Who else?"

"It's a big list, I said. Even if I took out all the Sam Pickleses, Jo-Jos, Jellies, Big Boogers, and—my favorite—Danny Dogs, the Ding-Dong Don—I'd be on the horn through lunch."

"I remember Danny. He wasn't always Ding-Dong. He got the clap, lost his marbles, thought he was Chuck Yeager, and broke the sound barrier sailing off the top floor of the Ferry Company warehouse. He might've had a little help with the launch."

"What is it with racket guys and STDs? Don't they ever use protection?"

"Only when they start their cars. Can you give me just the women?"

"That's easy. Mob's got a bulletproof glass ceiling. Not many X chromosomes on the payroll, only between the sheets. Frances Elizabeth Donella, age sixteen at the time of the report, known to subject socially. He should've been picked up for statutory rape."

"She sounds like the one Joey threw over Marcine for. Who else?"

"Iona Bernadette Cuneo Ballista, wife. Daughter of—"

"Check. Who else?"

"Lee Tan."

"Lee Tan? How'd a Lee Tan get in there?"

"Suspected business associate, it says here. 'See separate file.'"

"That'd be the Hong Kong connection. Old Joe Balls had the Asian heroin market all sewed up here, but the bottom fell out after the local black gangs crawled in bed with the Colombians. They sold it the way it came in Grosse Pointe and Bloomingham and stepped on it and sold it as crack on the West Side. Took about a week for the whole area to go on the cocaine standard."

"I was in training then. Who'd've thought those would be the good old days?"

"Any others?"

"That's it for women. You're putting a lot of store in your female-snitch theory."

"It's a place to start. I'll come by for the rest in case I stall. Can you get me a twenty on Donella and Tan?"

"No dice. Your solid's run out."

"Can I establish a line of credit?"

"With your rating?"

I felt my face get more haggard. "You're a twenty-minute egg, Marshal Thaler."

"Don't take too long getting around to picking up this list. If they find out I've got it and who it's for, they'll re-assign me to the air service. What are the odds I'll get Hawaii and not North Dakota?"

"I hear the Dakotas are nice this time of year."

"It wouldn't be this time of year."

I started to say something else, but I was speaking to an empty line.

There wasn't a Frances Donella in the directory. I hadn't expected there to be for several reasons, one being that if she'd stayed single she wouldn't advertise the fact to a predatory world. I tried Information, but the near-comatose party at the switchboard couldn't find her, listed or un-listed. There was a column of Lee Tans and I tried them all. All but two who answered were men, one of the women spoke next to no English, and the other sounded older than a thousand-year-old egg. I didn't ask either of them if she'd dealt dope in the '80s. All the globe-trotting involved would have been a young woman's game, and that second voice hadn't been young even all those years ago; I'd come to be a connoisseur of women middle-age on up. There's a lot of dickering even in controlled substances, and the owner of the first voice wouldn't have had the necessary language skills.

All this was theory, of course, just like the female-snitch angle. I wrote a question mark next to both names, along with one that hadn't answered. Detective work always be-gins with the metropolitan directory, but it almost never ends there.

More than ever I missed Barry Stackpole's cooperation. He'd have an entire file case on the U.S.–Asian heroin racket, with a drawer on Detroit subdivided by known deal-ers and a fat folder labeled TAN, LEE. Maybe it was a good thing in the long run. I'd become so dependent on him when the official sources were closed, I ought to have his name let-tered on my office door.

Then again, I needed a Ouija board to make contact with all the friends I had left.

I had a little more luck with the Iroquois Heights book, and a nice surprise. It's a slim pamphlet about the size and thickness of an auction catalogue. I don't know if it's sepa-rated from the Detroit-area listings by the Heights' choice or by Detroit's. No Lee Tans or Frances Donellas, but there was an M. Logan listed on Ottawa Place, a residential street located just off the main gut, a comfortable commute on foot to and from Iona's Simple Solutions; although from the look of Marcine's heels I doubted she went more than twenty yards on foot in any direction.

It needed confirmation, but I didn't call the number. The decorating firm didn't open for another hour, she'd still be at home if she wasn't a work freak, and I had nothing else to do all day but abuse my lungs with nicotine and probe at the knot on my jaw. I'm a work freak by necessity. I shaved and dressed and coaxed my Cutlass back from the dead.

Ottawa Place was a cul-de-sac. It didn't have to be, but dead-ending the street had landlocked the adjoining property, forcing the owner to sell it to the city for a bargain price. It was pretty, as those graft jobs often are, with tame trees and all the addresses stenciled on the curbs and square patches of lawn unencumbered by miniature windmills, iron jockeys, and other affronts to the antiblight ordinance: L-shaped ranch-styles, Frank Lloyd Wright knockoffs with low-pitched roofs and carports, and the house belonging to the address I'd found in the directory, a graceful stack of pre-aged brick built on two levels with Palladian windows, a covered arch opening onto the front door, and a slipper-shaped convertible parked face out in an open garage on the lower level. The car's yellow finish with black trim reminded me of a flashlight I'd once owned.

A stern sign warned the owners of the cars parked on the street that they had to move them to the opposite side between the hours of six P.M. and six A.M., a regulation drafted to discourage late-night dog-fighting, a colorful part of the recent local heritage. As a consequence there was plenty of space, and I turned around at the end of the street and found a spot with a straight shot at the Logan house next to a Neighborhood Watch sign with a picture of Boris Badenov. People hurrying to work generally ignore the cars parked on their side. I killed the engine and switched on the radio for company.

I don't have FM, and the pickings were lean. I browsed among right-wing talk shows, programs of Afro-Cuban jazz, oldies, oldies, oldies, hip-hop, country, hip-hop, country hip-hop, one lone liberal talk show loaded with static, and WJR, the all-commercials-all-the-time station, then snapped it off and listened to a morning TV news host chirruping through some open window telling me I could lose weight by pouring my cereal into smaller bowls. I flipped my visor down between me and the sun in the east, slid lower in the seat until my head rested against the back, and caught up on my smoking. I had both side windows open for the cross-draft and a parabolic patch of shade that in fifteen minutes would be a sweet memory. It was 8:30 by the dashboard clock and the weather guy had told me between pitches for bottled water and Sleep Number beds that the temperature at Metro Airport was eighty-five.

The lull between Detroit-bound commuters and the stiffs who worked locally ended just before the half hour. I wound up the window on the driver's side against the wallop of their passage, watched a slightly chubby blonde in a pink kimono and mules to match trying to wheel an empty trash can up her driveway while holding down her hem against the slipstream—a Vargas Girl moment—and saw a kid on a Segway make a nifty maneuver to avoid becoming a casualty of Overcaffeinated Motorist Syndrome. He turned the scooter in a circle and dismounted to give the driver the international sign of disapproval. As far as stakeouts go it was sweeps week.

The shade and traffic were gone along with my third cigarette when Marcine Logan came out her front door.

The sight made me grateful for something about Iroquois Heights for the first time, even if it was just a telephone book. She cherry-picked her way down a flagged flight of steps in a pair of red leather heels to the open garage. A long skirt, red also, gave me a flash of bare tanned thigh where a button-up slit was unfastened. The ends of a filmy red scarf floated outside the open neck of a white silk blouse. She carried a portfolio case open at the top, with double handles, and her golden-ash hair was pinned back loosely, tendrils riding the air. Kimono Girl had shown a lot more with less effect. Marcine was a treat at any age, but at forty-six she was vintage wine beautifully kept.

It was two minutes shy of nine o'clock. Either she was a valuable worker with special privileges or she had something on the boss.

Probably it was a little of both. Employers like Iona Cuneo usually found a way to get rid of chiselers with no redeeming qualities.

The yellow sports job started with a pleasant grumble and left the garage, the overhead door unfolding behind it. I slid down farther as she turned into the street, started the 455 with the somewhat louder treble of twin glass packs, then sat up and followed two blocks behind. I knew where she was going, with a two-point margin allowed for error; if I was wrong and I lost her, a vehicle like that wasn't hard to pick up again in a city of pickups and town cars with little variety in between.

She didn't have any surprises for me that morning. She turned into a parking garage with the entrance and exit in plain sight, came out on foot a few minutes later across from where I'd double-parked, swinging the portfolio and cracking her heels on the sidewalk toward Iona's Simple Solutions, where she went in and let the glass door glide shut behind her without stopping to look around.

When a space opened up I moved into it. Parking on that street was two hours and ruthlessly enforced. I was in for a long day of shuttling from one slot to another. Since I seldom know when I'm going to be forced to sit still for hours, I keep a store of energy bars and water in the car and a big empty coffee can for comfort. I fed the meter, walked to the end of the block and back to work the stiffness out of my joints, took off my coat and folded it on the backseat, and made myself at home in the passenger's seat in front. Passersby rarely give someone sitting there a second look, assuming he's waiting for the driver to come back from some errand.

I didn't know what I was waiting for or what I expected to see. Sometimes the work's like fishing, without the amenities.

I'd been there about an hour when I turned the radio back on to catch the news. The River Rouge police had recovered a woman's body found floating near the Ford plant early that morning. She was identified as Frances Elizabeth

Donella, forty-four, of Detroit. The Detroit Police Department was assisting with the investigation.

It took me a second to remember where I'd heard the name before. Then I ground the starter and swung back toward the big city, busting some lights along the way.

ELEVEN

I used up some of my minutes getting handed off until someone connected me with a sergeant I knew who told me I'd find Inspector John Alderdyce at the Wayne County Morgue. "Standing up," he assured me; there's always plenty of high comedy to be had at 1300.

Officially it's the Coroner's Court Building, but nobody's called it that since running boards went out of style. I parked in a loading zone on Lafayette, went through the emergency cards in the glove compartment until I found a medical one with a serpent-and-staff, and fixed it to my visor so it could be seen through the windshield. The gag almost never spared me a ticket, but it usually slowed down the tow truck. I walked three blocks to Brush and entered the tidy corner building shaped like the prow of an ocean liner that some visitors mistook for the Detroit Athletic Club.

The clerk at the desk took my name, found Alderdyce's in the day register, spoke over a telephone, and had me sign in. I stuck the pass he gave me in a pocket and went to the viewing room.

In recent years they'd furnished the waiting room out-side with a closed-circuit monitor for friends and family to identify the deceased without actually going into cold stor-age, but medical students from Wayne State University gave it more of a workout observing autopsies over a sack lunch. Today the room was deserted and the screen was black. I went on in without knocking, into a dry cold that always smelled like ammonia and formaldehyde to me, even though experts claim the chemicals have long since been replaced by something more efficient and odorless. Anyway it's a less sinister smell than the underlay of open carcasses, like the back room of a butcher shop.

John Alderdyce stood conversing in murmurs with a Pakistani medical examiner in gold-rimmed glasses and a white coat across one of the sheet-covered tables that took up most of the space in a room the size of a handball court. He was darker than the M.E. and twice as large. He wore a chocolate brown suit, tailored by one of the Chosen, with a thin lavender pinstripe and a shirt-and-tie set that matched the stripe. It was an elegant package for something that ought to have come in a crate. You could pound Swiss steak on his forehead and strike matches off his cheekbones.

In contrast to the lumps under the other sheets, the one on the table where the pair was gathered lay uncovered to the waist. If this was Frances Donella, she hadn't aged as well as either Marcine Logan or Iona Cuneo Ballista, but then I wasn't seeing her under the best circumstances. They'd pulled her out of the water before bloating, but the immersion had turned her skin slate blue. Her breasts were empty flaps and violent patches of postmortem lividity made broad angry streaks across her puffy face. The vicious black ragged scar of a first-class job of throat-cutting may have had something to do with those. Her hair was leaden gray, plastered to her forehead and scalp.

I played with a cigarette. I couldn't light it there, but the stage business made my fingers busy and kept them from shaking. Lying in state in parlors, the dead looked as if they were sleeping, and stumbled upon unexpectedly in woods and bobbing in currents they looked like mannequins, but in that whitewashed room in halogen light they just looked dead.

"Who ID'd her?" I said by way of greeting. My voice fell automatically to a murmur.

Alderdyce worked his shoulders, loosening the muscles that bunched there like fallen boulders. "Who's asking, you or your bankroll?"

"Me, of course. I'm a cadaver buff, can't get enough of that necro rush. Lovecraft and Poe are Mother Goose to me."

The medical examiner nodded, acknowledging a comrade. They make Trekkies look like society.

"You're babbling. Sure sign of concussion." Alderdyce reached across the corpse, took my chin between a thumb and forefinger the size of steam pistons, and turned the rotten patch his way. "Past life catch up with you?"

"Feels like more than just one. I must've been Stalin last time around."

"You're getting too old to keep on running into bridges. I hear a man's pension goes further in Central America."

"Farther." I tipped my head back, freeing myself from his grip. He could crush a hockey puck when he was distracted. "I didn't know inspectors sat in on floaters. You get at least five a month, like phases of the moon. What's the attraction?"

"I get interested when the phase in question used to bump pelvises with Joey Ballistic. What about you?"

"I heard about it in my car. I thought there might be a nickel in it. The dog days are hell on private work. All the party wives and husbands in heat are with the kids in Florida, taking advantage of the summer rates."

"You don't do divorce work and you don't chase coroner's vans. Take another swing."

"Okay, I was kidding about the wives and husbands. It's still my slow season. If she had family or a boyfriend, they might want to know something you cops aren't releasing."

"Like who put her in the water?"

"Like what she was doing before she got put in the water. Knowing about those last hours is important to survivors."

"And you're just the character that can get us to open up when the press can't."

"I'm just the character who knows what questions to ask."

Alderdyce's brain peered out at me through the holes punched in his skull. Then he turned to the Pakistani and spoke as if I wasn't there. "Two hours, you said?"

"Around that. Much more and the tissues saturate and they sink. Then it's three days before the gas brings them back to the surface. No decomposition here. Rigor's still in place." He flicked a finger at her chest. It made a noise like a plank, only less pleasant. "I wish they could all be floaters; it makes the job simple. I wouldn't put her in there much before two."

The inspector asked me what I'd been doing at two A.M.

I pictured myself gargling Scotch to relieve mandibular stress.

"Sleeping."

"Alone?"

"I said it's my slow season."

"Stackpole said he spent the night at home. I thought you single guys lived more gaudy."

"I don't get out much lately. I'm getting brittle." So Barry had told the cops he hadn't left his house. I started to put the shopworn cigarette between my lips, but my mouth was so dry I thought it would snatch away skin when I took it out. I put it back in the pack. "You talked to Barry?"

"First call I made when we pulled her driver's license out of her pocket. He had a bag on. He said he didn't know any Donellas. He didn't sell it, but I let him think he did, this pass. She was never public record, but the bureaucracy's no proof against a newshawk like him. I don't guess you forgot his interest in Ballista is personal."

"Did Joey identify her?"

"Her pimp did, after her sheet came up and we brought him in. She fell on hard nails after she and Joey split, just about the time he went away for that fireworks stunt. She started out working for an escort service and wound up on the Michigan Avenue assembly line, thumbing rides with her hips along with the rest. Priors up the ass for soliciting and possession, went into the program the first time to stay out of County. She lasted about a day. Two uniforms were waiting for her when she got back to her apartment. She got six months in DeHoCo. Didn't learn a trade there, looks like. I never saw one go straight outside a movie theater."

"Holding the pimp?"

"Would I be spending any time in this human landfill if we could bend his alibi?"

"Who's sweating Joey?"

"Lieutenant Hornet, but he's just collecting paperwork. Joey's on an electronic tether. We talked to his P.O. He hasn't stirred from his crib in days."

"I knew Hornet when he was a sergeant. I thought he quit the department."

"As good as, until he transferred back to Homicide from the mayor's security detail. They're all fat, have you noticed? Hizzoner's diet plan: How to look skinny without losing a pound."

"It's not working. Talk to Joey's wife?"

"She told us to call her lawyer. We'll run it out, but I don't see a motive after all these years and her and Joey separated. Also this isn't a woman's kind of kill unless you count shot-putters and body builders."

"How much upper-body strength does it take to slit a woman's throat?"

"Who says her throat was slit?"

I set my teeth and looked again at the wound. It looked slit to me.

I said, "It looks slit to me."

"Tell him, since he's here. He's an awful pest."

The medical examiner touched his glittering glasses. "Color's a dead giveaway. Excuse the expression. Blue skin means cyanosis. Not enough oxygen in the blood. That takes place when something happens to prevent it from getting there." He slid a finger with a very clean nail along the top edge of the gash. "The purple contusions are caused by ligatures. This woman was strangled."

"Hanging?" I asked.

"That diagnosis is inconsistent with the lack of ligature marks on her wrists. When you hang someone against his will it's advisable to prevent him from grabbing the rope and holding on until help arrives. It's possible our victim was insensible, but I can't comment on whether she was sedated until the toxicity report comes back from the lab. Absenting hanging by suicide"—he smiled shyly, touching his glasses—"one seldom if ever releases oneself afterward and throws oneself in the river—I'd say a garrote was involved."

I took out a fresh cigarette and started to ruin it. "That's a Mafia signature. Anyone else and it's infringement of copyright. It puts Joey back in the race."

"If he hired it, he still needed a reason," Alderdyce said. "He'd have to be as bugs as his old man was to risk it over an old grudge."

I said, "I hear he's in bad health. Maybe he's putting his affairs in order."

"*Where'd* you hear he's in bad health?"

I looked down at the cigarette. I'd nearly walked right into it. That clip I'd taken must have knocked my brain off one of its rubber mounts. "I heard he almost clocked out in the federal pen."

"I heard it was more than almost," Alderdyce said after a moment. He sounded disappointed. Whether it was because the same rumor I'd heard had been overly optimistic or because I'd sidestepped the snare he'd set, I couldn't tell. "He got well enough to finish out his time. Anyway, he's not acting like a man waiting for a shovel. Guess who's representing him now?"

I looked at him, shook my head.

He told me, watching my face.

"Lefty Lucy," I pursed my lips. "I thought she only stood up for anarchists."

"Everyone's changing lays this year. Look at you: You hear a siren, you take off after it like a greyhound. The point is no one retains a red-hot to dig him out of a pile of legal trouble, then turns around and makes the red-hot's job twice as tough by ordering a hit. Our friend here would say the diagnosis is inconsistent with the sense God gave a cockroach."

"Maybe he's counting on you thinking that way."

"He doesn't think cops are that smart, and he's right. We never look an open-and-shut case in the mouth."

I agreed, but not for that reason. I looked at the M.E., who appeared a little hurt to have heard himself mocked; considering the job, their hides are surprisingly thin. "What'd he use, wire?" I asked. "Looks like it cut deep."

"Five centimeters." The dark little man brightened. "I used a magnet to extract any particles, but that's only a short-cut if it was steel; magnets don't attract copper or brass or aluminum. I haven't peeled back the epidermis yet, but I doubt I'll find metal. My guess is it was monofilament, thin but extremely strong. It wouldn't have existed even ten years ago. Chemists have made some real strides developing high-test line for the fishing industry."

"Fishline?"

He nodded, beaming now. A dull bell swung in a dim room I didn't visit very often. I wondered what it was shouting about.

TWELVE

heard that," Alderdyce said.

I said, "I didn't say anything."

"That's what I mean. When you're not talking you're thinking."

"Sorry. I didn't see the sign."

"Department shrink says I'm territorial," he said. "I told him, 'The taxpayers are paying you to tell cops they're territorial?' I like to bust my own cherries. When I find out some other john got there first I tend to become woolly."

"I've noticed. I didn't want to say anything."

He looked at the medical examiner, who was busy studying old needle tracks on the inside of Frances Donella's left elbow. He turned away, placing a massive shoulder in the space between. It seemed an unnecessary exclusion, even if it had been effective in those close quarters; the little man's interest was strictly horizontal. "Mary Ann Thaler's been shaking the Ballista family tree. Care to tell me why before I call her?"

I didn't hesitate more than a nanosecond, but it hanged

me just the same. "Downtown's just a gossip factory, isn't it? I'd be better off confiding in a bridge party."

"What'd you think it was, Most Holy Trinity?" He waited.

"I'm working it," I said. "The customer's an officer of the court. What's that buy me in the way of attorney-client privilege?"

"Not a goddamn thing." His voice went up two octaves; he couldn't manage falsetto even then, but the effect was sufficiently mocking. " 'Lefty Lucy. I thought she only stood up for anarchists.' Jesus. When you run a bluff you ought to look at who you're running it on. So you're hanging with the wiseguys now. I should've seen it when you came in wearing that suit."

"Nice try, Sherlock. The suit isn't that good." But he'd picked up quicker than expected. For a man who was all bone and muscle and elephant hide, John Alderdyce was as sensitive as a tuning fork.

"If you think you can stonewall me, you don't know stone. Stackpole plus Thaler equals Walker. When the media weevils make the connection between another dead hooker and the Combination—which they will, the minute some thirteen-year-old superstar isn't going into or coming out of rehab—I'm not telling them we're working on some promising leads. I'll say we've got a material witness in custody. Stackpole's one of them—no help—Lettermore's Lettermore—major case against the city—but a P.I.'s just a snoop however his jacket hangs. How you figure to earn your per diem in county?"

"I've done it before. And as long as I'm working for Lettermore, I'm Lettermore too. You think she'd dump me after all the time she's served for contempt?"

The room got quieter, and it was full of stiffs. He nodded finally, due to some shift in tectonic plates. "Okay, pal. You're Lettermore."

His tone wouldn't have stirred the surface of a reflecting pool. Even the M.E. responded, looking up at him through his spotless lenses.

I shrugged. It beat screaming and running. I gave it to him—the interview, that is. I hadn't worked a fourteen-hour shift to give it away. When I finished the silence was complete, until he broke it over his knee.

"Horseshit. If you can make a first offender out of Joey Ballistic, I can get up a softball team out of this room."

"I didn't draw up the plan."

"How's Stackpole taking it? Ah. Mystery solved. He slugs good for a cripple. You're usually better at keeping up your right."

"He slugs good for Sugar Ray. I saw it coming and I stood in front of it. I figured it would help sober him up for the drive home."

"When was this?"

"Last night, early." I'd seen that coming too. I wouldn't alibi him, but I wouldn't bend his alibi either. Not that it mattered. He'd still had time to find Joey's old girlfriend and deal her out of the hand.

Alderdyce seemed to be thinking in the same direction; anyway he didn't call me out. "Think he did it? She might have exonerated Joey."

"If he did, it's out of character. He lost a cushy TV job for refusing to deep-six evidence that a major sponsor was in bed with the Guerrera brothers."

"That wasn't personal."

"Make it personal, then. What's he gain by letting who-ever really blew him up off the hook?"

"What's he gain by coldcocking you when you told him you're working for Joey's lawyer?"

"He was drunk."

"He didn't have much time to dry out between you and Frances."

"It's an expensive proposition trying to get Barry drunk enough to drop a syllable. I've seen him drunker than that—drunker than last night—but his personality doesn't change. He'd've been just as sore at me sober, under the circumstances, though it might've ended in words instead of a dinger, but even then it's a tall stretch from there to throttling a woman with fishline. An around-the-world stretch."

"A guy can go off his nut for all sorts of reasons. Maybe he had a flashback. Among you vets that's like the common cold."

"I was wondering when you'd draw that card. That one never goes stale. Maybe we should all be on a register, like sex offenders." I hadn't time to count to ten, so I kicked a leg of the table. The pain in my big toe gave me something else to think about. I took in a draft of the vile mortuary air and let it go. The world listed right, left, then wobbled on. "Say he made the stretch. If he popped anyone, it'd be Joey. A thing like that's more cost effective in the long run."

He nodded. The Fisher Building swayed, too, in gale winds. "I withdraw that flashback crack; strike it from the record. Like cops don't have to face the same shit. He's still our hot lead till he cools off."

The M.E. spoke up. I think we'd both forgotten he was

there. "I'd pay him a visit, get a look at his hands. High-test cuts both ways. If the killer didn't wear gloves, his palms will look like the victim's neck."

I said, "It's looking more and more like the underworld. Tradition's the only reason anyone would take the trouble, with so many guns floating around."

"I can think of plenty of reasons," Alderdyce said. "Putting it on the underworld, for starters. That takes us back to Stackpole. He's been lugging a grudge since before Japanese cars."

"Which takes us back to why didn't he just do Joey. Even if he wanted him living, wearing cotton drawers for life and wishing they were silk, he had to know Joey was wearing an ironclad alibi around his ankle."

"Well, is it all right with you if I don't take him off redial just yet?"

"It's your case. Mine's to get that tether off Joey."

"I hope it takes you as long as it took us to put it on."

I called Lucille from the car to bring her up to speed. She was eating at her desk and stopped crunching just once during the report. When I finished she swallowed and said, "I doubt Joey's got the strength anymore for that kind of work, even if he found a way to slip the leash. You think this Donella woman was the snitch?"

"That's what I'm on my way to find out. Whoever killed her broke the seal of Detective Severin's confessional."

I didn't tell her any more than that. It saved having to explain myself if my gnawing hunch didn't pan out.

When I'd entered the morgue the sky had been as clear as if someone had drawn a scraper across it. Now it was low and dirty and pregnant with severe weather. A rumble of thunder that was having trouble finding a place to stop said someone was getting it and we were next. Meteorologists live for days like that. I gave up looking for a program of music without breathless interruptions, turned off the radio, and leaned over to crank down the window on the passenger's side to relieve pressure. The air conditioner had quit working, they don't make that kind now for ecological reasons, and when I had time to have it replaced I couldn't afford to and when I could afford to I hadn't time. The slipstream lifted the cover of the county atlas on the passenger's seat and shook it. I had the route down now and didn't need it; I just hadn't gotten around to putting it away after the last trip.

This time I wasn't dressed like the natives. I jerked loose my tie and threw it in the back on top of my coat, steered with my elbow while I unbuttoned my cuffs and turned them back. The air combed the hair on my wrists, evaporating the beads of perspiration from the ends. The students and unemployed laborers were shut in from the coming weather and pedestrians scooted along hoping to make shelter before it came, leaning into the stiffening wind. Part of the *Free Press* sports section leapt up onto my windshield and refused to leave until I snatched it away with a wiper.

I turned them on again just outside the city limits. It started with a handful of big clear circles against the glass like silicone, but by the time I got the second window back up, my sleeve was drenched to the elbow and the county atlas was plastered to the seat. I was moving west, the weather was moving east, and the impact of our combined momentum rocked the car and tried to turn it around on top of a patch of standing water the size of a retention pool. I eased up on the accelerator, letting the car straighten itself out with a light touch on the wheel, and tugged on the lights against the sudden dark. Lightning fractured the sky. The thunderclap that came hard on its heels sounded like someone pounding the roof with both fists. Baby tooth–size hailstones rataplanned on the vinyl and jumped and skidded on the hood.

Motorists who feared for their sheetmetal had pulled over in the shelter of underpasses. A touring party of motorcyclists with bedrolls on their bikes had parked under one and stood on the apron bumming dry cigarettes off one another. A pair of flashers tilted at a crazy angle showed where a car had slid into a ditch. I called 911 to help out and for once got a dispatcher who hadn't flunked three civil service exams before getting lucky on the fourth. The traffic slowed to forty-five. I slowed with it. Taillights and license plates sprang into my low beams out of nowhere.

When the windshield steamed over I turned on the heater and blower. I'd gotten a little chilled from the soaking and it felt cozy at first, but then sweat broke in a torrent and I turned them off. The car had become a diving bell, liquid all around. The hard heavy hissing was monotonous, hypnotic, broken by brief eerie silences that switched on and then off as I plunged under overpasses. I'd traveled through three seasons in ten minutes.

And then I was out of it, as suddenly as I was in. The front was moving rapidly, like an irrigation boom swinging across a field. Blue sky gleamed hard through holes torn in the overcast, a pond that had been ten acres of soybeans was flat and placid. I changed lanes to avoid suspicious puddles, but slowing down to take one easily when cars were passing me I still managed to chip a tooth on the mother of all potholes. Almost immediately I picked up a vibration that would add the cost of wheel alignment to my expenses.

Out in country the worst of the damage revealed itself like an unhealed cut. I went partly up a bank to get around a shattered limb lying across a rural road, and with the windows open I heard the angry throat-clearing of chain saws. A row of electric poles two feet thick had been sheared off eight feet above the ground and although clusters of clouds still cast their shadows I drove through an entire township without seeing a light burning anywhere. A group of men in shirtsleeves and women in shapeless summer dresses stood in front of a house looking at a tree that had caved in part of the roof. A line of cars and pickups parked on the edge of the road showed where they'd stopped to get out and gawk or offer help. It was one of those fierce little disasters we get throughout the summer, too common an occurrence to inspire charity drives.

From Pinckney on, the locals seemed to have dodged the bullet. The village appeared orderly. Puddles were running off the edge of the two-lane blacktop that led from it and broken branches lay on lawns, but a bulb glowed in an open garage. Power generators have gotten to be essential equipment out there where Detroit Edison can take days to put the residents back on the grid, but the noisy things were silent. Storms tend to run in troughs, pounding one side of the street while people sit in sunlight on porches on the other side, watching them. I wondered which side my house was on back in town.

Randy's Marina was one of the lucky ones. The lights were still racing around the edge of the sign in front and although the lake behind it was choppy and pewterish under a cloud cover the long building looked as calm as a toad under its slant roof. The canoes and kayaks tethered there were leaning against one another and looking put out about it, but apart from that the heavy wind had let the place alone, even if it had put a slack in the business trade. The thirty-seven-year-old Ford pickup was the only vehicle in sight.

It was a homicide investigation now. I clipped on the .38 and pulled out my shirttail to cover it.

The mouths of the fish heads nailed to the outside wall hung open as before, the bass like comical fat men in Stage One denial and disbelief, the pike with their nasty alligator snouts and rows of razor teeth biding their time waiting for one last bite. The bell attached to the screen door raised its redundant alarm when it banged shut behind me.

Inside nothing much stirred. The bamboo shades were drawn at the back, parsing the drab outside light into thin blades that tickled the polish of a plastic lure and separated tracked-in beach sand into individual grains. My pupils worked it, a little slower each day like the rest of my reflexes. I smelled pine scent, nightcrawlers burrowing blindly in pots of moist black earth, the vanilla tinge of gun oil, and something else, a harsh, burnt something that puckered my nostrils like lye in a bed of charcoal, only not so homely and harmless. My hand found the checked butt of the Chief's Special and broke it loose.

Randolph Severin, Detroit Police Detective Retired, sat on his tall stool behind the glass counter as if he'd never left it, but he wasn't messing with his ball of snarled fishline today. His horned hands hung loose between his thick thighs and his brush-cut head rested its chin on his collarbone. His hard belly in the green workshirt with RANDY'S MARINA on a pocket patch pressed against the edge of the counter, holding him more or less upright. I bent my knees a little to get a better angle on his face. Something had made a blue-black hole an inch and a half above the bridge of his nose, as round and as nearly perfect as if it had been a carpenter bee. There didn't seem to be any need to disturb evidence looking for a pulse.

I straightened and looked through the glass in front of him. All those guns. The irony in the air was as thick as the stink of spent powder.

THIRTEEN

I worked fast. Now that the blow was over it wouldn't be long before business picked up.

The investigation took me behind the counter. The back of his head was in worse shape than the front, the gray hair dark and matted, with splinters of polished skull splayed out and the first fly of many busy in the center. That last fact spared me touching his skin to test for body temperature. In half an hour, maybe less, they'd be swarming. In that country, the flies gather even before the reporters.

I turned my back to the door, not without a prickling sensation. Something had broken the shade behind him, although not so badly you'd notice it if you weren't looking for it. I found the string and pulled, using my shirttail to frustrate the fingerprint team. With the shade raised the damage was more apparent. The bullet had punched a hole in the window on its way out, not nearly as symmetrical as the one it had made going in, but not big enough to suggest a piece of lead beaten out of shape by thick skull; a hunk like that would have shattered the pane. Instead it was just

starred. A jacketed round, copper or steel, probably belonging to a .45 pistol. The ball of my thumb went through it
without touching the edge.

An expert would determine the trajectory with measur-
ing tape or a length of cord. Not having either I put my eye
to the hole, a natural enough gesture for one in my profession. It seemed to line up with a red log house sprawled on
the opposite side of the lake. No eyewitness there, or in a
boat in between, with the shade down. No earwitness either,
if it had happened during the storm. In any case a single
shot wouldn't have caused much of a stir out there where
gun sales kept a dealer in fair-weather supplies afloat in the
off season. I lowered the shade.

There was no sign of the Gordian knot that Severin had
been struggling with yesterday, and I wasn't about to leave
any more DNA behind than I had to opening drawers and
cabinets. If my hunch was worth anything it wouldn't be
there anyway. He'd have ditched it in the river—with
Frances Donella's body—along with all the tales it could
tell.

Randolph Severin didn't have to be the one who'd done
that. All I had to go on was a description of the murder
weapon, the project he'd been working on all the time we'd
spoken, and the possibility he'd put Joey Ballista in a frame
all those years ago based on information he'd gotten from
Joey's teenage mistress that might not hold up if she were
brought in and questioned now that the case was under re-
view. It would mean the loss of his pension and probable
jail time, but it was all guesswork on my part. I hadn't liked
him. Most of the people I didn't like didn't turn out to be
murderers.

Except someone else who seemed to have liked him less than I did had beaten me to him by minutes.

I put my hands on my hips and sucked my teeth. I wasn't wondering what came next, just putting it off. I'd congratulated myself prematurely. I had to touch him to inspect his palms. Only the backs of his hands showed where they dangled between his thighs, sprinkled with silvery hairs that reminded me of fishing line.

The palms were warm when I turned them up, slightly moist, and as unmarked as a baby's, although no baby's were ever that thick. The layers of callus might have prevented them from getting slashed up strangling someone with a loop of thin filament, and it wouldn't have taken much effort for a solid type like him to choke the life out of a female heroin addict. The medical examiner in Detroit hadn't said anything about that. She'd have put up a fight if she wasn't too far gone on dope, in which event there would be blood and skin under her nails. He hadn't mentioned that either, and I hadn't thought to ask. Both questions would be answered when the tests came back.

Returning to the front of the counter I stooped for another look at the wound. No contact burns on the skin. That made sense, if you understood splash patterns and didn't want to be pulled over for a broken taillight with a Rorschach pattern of hemoglobin and cerebral fluid on your shirt. Every year brings a bigger caliber to the personal firearms market—another few centimeters and they'll come with air bags to absorb the recoil—but a .45 is plenty of gun even by elephant-load standards. Most people just bring back an axe from the hardware store.

I went to the door, took my revolver back out, and

turned, straightening my arm at shoulder level with the sight lined up on where Severin's forehead would have been when he looked up to see who'd entered. Some bully shot for a weapon not designed for competition, but if you were good enough it spared you coming in all the way, shedding hair and skin cells and God and criminal science knew what else.

That was the extent of my forensics education. I didn't watch enough TV. I returned the .38 to its clip, dropped my shirttail back over it, and smeared the handle on the outside of the screen door with my palm, leaving more evidence than I removed, but I was already on record as having visited earlier and I didn't want my prints too close to the top.

The fish heads stared back at me with bulging, lidless eyes. They'd resisted evolution for twenty million years. They weren't about to give up what they'd seen under routine interrogation.

I drove back the way I came, passing a short SUV headed toward the marina with fishing rods sticking out the open back window. I hoped that was as close as I'd cut it.

FOURTEEN

The dinner stop I made was just a matter of physics. I had no appetite—a hamburger burned to anything less than a crisp would have spoiled what remained of a day that had started out with so much promise—but I wasn't sure when I'd eaten last, and the plans I'd made for the evening didn't include getting too drunk too soon. I was getting too old to camp out on the floor two nights in a row. I was getting too old for many things, murder being just one. I had a bowl of lentil soup and a fistful of crackers in the extended strip mall that had evolved from the city of Wixom, a turnaround off I-96, and stuck the toothpick back into my tuna salad on whole wheat to mark my passage.

Next door to that polished little chain place I bought a bottle of premium Scotch from a drugstore clerk who looked from my face to the video camera to make sure it was working, and scuttled on out huddling my prize in its paper bag. I didn't think I could face the bottle of rug cleaner back at the house, and if there was ever a time I could charge liquor to expenses, this was it. I hadn't known Frances

Elizabeth Donella. I hadn't liked Randolph Severin, and I'd passed that dangerous point marked with orange floats where stumbling over corpses made me question my career choice, but the logical conclusion of the chain of reasoning that linked retired cop to former mistress to friend of youth and middle age put the golden shine on oblivion.

Back in the hutch I ferreted out my best old-fashioned glass, triangulated like the mullioned windows at Balmoral, with a heavy leaded base, chucked in four ice cubes, and poured in two fingers, filling the rest of the space with water, the way they say Sinatra preferred to drink his Jack, and sipped at it in my armchair. It tasted like Scotch-flavored water. I lost a little respect then for the Chairman of the Board; but then the closest he'd come to homicide was a night on the town with Sam Giancana and Willie Moretti, and anyway, music was his thing. I put on the *Wee Small Hours* album on vinyl—the suicide sides—then replaced it with *Come Fly With Me*, and replaced the contents of my glass with weapons-grade rotgut from the plastic jug. It wasn't a night for drinking Noel Coward style.

The musicians I admired believed you could only find truth once you've obliterated reason. Miles Davis had taken it too far, pumping his veins full of the poison that would have put Frances Donella in the River Rouge or someplace just as corrupt regardless of other circumstances, so that you could only enjoy his later stuff if you were as wasted as he was when he'd recorded it, but there's something to be said for altering your perception away from the lineal.

Half a bottle past ten, I had it. I took one sip more and then it was gone. I had to stumble back into the kitchen for a refresher to retrieve it. Barry was right; it was possible to drink yourself sober, just as Jack Dempsey said a boxer could knock a man unconscious, then back awake. I knew then what had bothered me most about the tableau at Randy's Marina.

I'd spent less than fifteen minutes with the man, but in that time I'd learned that he was not the kind who could rest contented with his own company, doing nothing but contemplating space. He'd spent our entire interview wrestling with the problem of obtaining a few yards of salable fishline from a tangle that couldn't have put more than twenty dollars in his cash drawer if he managed to straighten out enough of it to satisfy a customer. When fate came calling, it would find him, if not engaged in that challenge, dusting his merchandise or detailing the keys of his cash register with a toothbrush. It wouldn't have found him sitting empty-handed on his stool.

I should've prowled the drawers and cabinets looking for that bit of line. It wouldn't be there, but looking would've spared me the possibility of following a lead into a barricade. I should've signed up for health insurance back when I healed more quickly. I should've bought Microsoft at five.

Mostly I should've let my cell phone lose its charge before Lucille Lettermore called me to discuss a job.

The bruise, I saw when I found my focus in the bathroom mirror, had developed a yellow streak. It seemed to have locked into my emotions like a mood ring. I wanted to run from the case. Instead I sprawled out on my back in my clothes on the bedspread and didn't stir a hair until the sun battered its way in. I knew I hadn't, because the squat glass stood undisturbed on my chest where I'd rested it, with the melted ice turning the contents the color of pus. The movers were thumping around behind my eyes and my lips made a sound like cellophane tearing when I pulled them apart. All my old friends had entered a conspiracy to spoil my mornings.

Soap and caffeine helped. My headache had subsided to a half-pleasant dull hum, like a faulty transformer, and I called Lucille to set up an appointment. She bumped a DUIL to the afternoon and scribbled me in. She didn't ask why the face-to-face. Something in my voice must have told her it wasn't a conversation for the telephone.

When I got there she let me right on in. She hadn't kept a receptionist since the last one had sold her out to a tabloid. "What the hell happened to you?" she asked. "On second thought, don't tell me. Just put it on the sheet." She took up her post behind the plate-glass desk. Today the blazer was lime green, with a pale green silk scarf knotted around her short stout neck. It made her look like a tortoise.

I sat down. The analog clocks on the shelves behind her ticked out of sync; the digitals were sullenly silent. My nerves lay on top of my skin and I massaged my left cheek to interrupt the break dance that was taking place there. I crossed my legs. Wearing my pants as pajamas hadn't done the creases any favors, but I had on a clean shirt and a fresh tie and the styptic seals felt reassuringly tight over the evidence of the morning's bloodbath. Yesterday I'd considered switching to an electric shaver. Today a full beard sounded reasonable.

She opened. "Talk to Severin?"

"The day before yesterday it was like playing pinochle with a trout. It was a little more so yesterday."

I'd triggered something. She was sitting straight in her chair, but now the guy wires tightened a quarter-inch. She'd listened to thousands of hours of testimony ready to swoop down like an owl when something stirred outside its hole. From turtle to bird of prey wasn't much of a stretch for her. "How bad?"

"It can't get any worse for him."

"Murder?"

"It was an awkward angle to shoot himself, but it's been done. Then he got up and went out back and threw the gun in the lake and came back inside and sat down and waited for me to find him. Maybe he stopped to wipe his feet."

"No chance it was accidental? Someone's always shooting at something out there in the sticks."

"That's been done too, but I'm pretty sure it was a forty-five or something close, which is an effective weapon up to about twenty feet. Whoever fired it had to be standing right in front of the building aiming right at it. You might as well do murder if you're going to flaunt all the laws against that."

"Is this fun for you?"

"Sure. Every time I feel up a stiff I bust a gut."

"I didn't mean it that way. It's just that you can't say anything in one word when ten will do just as well."

"Sorry. I know you measure out minutes in greenbacks. You think I'd be used to it by now, but every time something like this happens I come away rickety. I'm this close to taking the veil." I laid it all out then. She sat without blinking or taking notes. Records were poison. Parties armed with search warrants seldom called before dropping in.

"That's a leap, from seeing fishing line in a marina to

putting it around Frances Donella's throat with Severin on the other end," she said when I'd wrapped up.

"I admit it. The medical examiner's words put it in my head. There isn't anything there, except someone else put a bullet in his when I was on my way out to ask him about it."

"He worked more than one case when he was a cop. You said he wasn't folksy. Anyone with a gripe or who just didn't like him could've done it. Don't knock coincidence, Amos. A couple of dozen people are walking around free right now because I had faith in it and sold it in court."

"I'd take it around the block, if one of Joey Ballista's mistresses didn't run into a coincidence of her own the same day I heard her name for the first time."

"That doesn't make her Severin's snitch."

"Every hooker and doper has her time, but let's take *my* theory around the block. Cops don't like gangsters. Cop gets gangster's girl to give him cause to investigate gangster, rigs evidence against him—evidence which conveniently gets lost in the system—case comes back to haunt cop, cop kills girl, using a well-known mob method to divert suspicion. Mob takes that in bad spirit and kills cop, using the *coup de grâce*, which is another mob method tested by time." I put a finger to my forehead and flicked my thumb.

"Fits the facts. One wonders why the cops don't recruit more goons to help them solve crimes on the microwave principle."

"The timeline's tight, but I like it better than cosmic forces moving into place like a conga dance."

"There's another theory that fits the facts just as well."

I nodded, scratching my cheek, which scratched back.

"Someone who had even more interest in seeing Joey behind bars kills snitch to keep her from changing her story, then the cop to keep him from doing the same once she hits the headlines. There's no reason to assume, given his sources, he didn't have all the names he needed or know where to find them after all this time."

"Is that why you didn't call the cops?"

"No. They'd have it in less than half an hour anyway. I'd had my fill of law enforcement for one day. Those county types resent it when crooks from the city litter their scenic roads with corpses. When they get a look at my credentials and find out where I keep my office, they transfer that resentment to me. I'll wait till the case lands back in Detroit, where the cops hate me for myself."

She had a computer on a stand perpendicular to the desk with a monitor as thick as a dime. I'd never seen her use it, but she attacked the keys with professional fingers. After a minute or so she said, "Township constable, does the preliminary for the county sheriffs. Homer S Bruno; no period after the *S*."

"You're kidding."

"Nope. Family name lasts as long as the family, and someone has to be called Homer or we'll be up to our asses in Brians and Michaels and Joshuas more than we are already. Know what no period after the *S* means?"

"It means he got it out of a gumball machine the first time he filled out a credit app. Corporate doesn't like it when you don't have a middle name. I don't know what Harry S Truman's excuse was." I crossed my legs the other way to make both creases match. "It wasn't the Homer or the Bruno or even the *S* I thought you were kidding about.

I thought constables went out of style along with undertakers and barbers."

"They're phasing them out in this state, on a retirement basis, just like they did with justices of the peace. I pled my first case before one of the quaint old charlatans." She shut down the computer and turned back my way. "Your eyes look like shit."

"You should see them from this side."

"Seems to me I heard that in a western."

I shrugged. No veteran will admit he sat through a movie with Jane Fonda in the cast. "All I can say is don't believe everything Frank Sinatra said when he wasn't singing."

She was reading my mind. All the good lawyers pretend they can, but only the best manage to pull it off. "Barry Stackpole's a vet, like you. He'd know his way around an automatic pistol, and he's been studying the Mafia long enough to get a handle on the garrote."

"I don't make him for it."

"Not the violent type? Who put that mouse on your jaw?"

"I'm not an eighty-pound hooker."

She was looking at my eyes again. I guessed they weren't hazel anymore. "What've you been drinking lately?"

"Scotch and water. That water's lethal stuff. I can see why the global warming people are so nervous."

"It should be recalled. All the same," she said, returning to topic, "I'm guessing Barry's your next visit, if only to get a look at his hands. He probably wore gloves, you know. Most murderers are stupid, but if they all were, you and I would be out of a job."

"Speak for yourself. My specialty's missing persons. He wears a glove on one hand most of the time, to disguise the missing fingers. I guess he's still sensitive about it after all these years."

"You think?"

I shook my head. The nerve in my cheek had flattened out finally. "I forgot to mention there were no contact burns on Severin's forehead. A forty-five throws plenty of flame. You have to be good with a heavy caliber to pull off a shot between the eyes from much farther than five feet. The kick throws you off. I don't think Barry's that good. It takes practice, and he spends most of his time either at a computer or burrowing into the organization pretending to be harmless."

"Maybe he was aiming at his heart."

"He'd have used less gun and taken out the guesswork. Anyway, if he has any doubts about Joey's guilt, it means the one who blew him to pieces was never called to account. That's the one he'd turn vigilante on."

"So no visit to Barry."

"A visit to Barry, to make sure I didn't overlook any bases. It can wait. I'm still interested in the women in Joey's life. I'm not convinced it was Severin did Donella. If it was someone else, he might've jumped to the wrong conclusion on which one turned in Joey. That puts all his women at risk."

She drummed her fingertips on the glass desk. Most who suffered from the imperfect human condition would have left wet smears; not Lefty Lucy. People who don't sweat make me nervous. They're like a pressure cooker with no safety valve. "I've always been aware of your Walter

Raleigh complex. I can overlook it, same as anorexia or a gambling problem, so long as it doesn't interfere with my case. I need to know if you're working for me or spreading yourself between Iona and Marcine and a mud puddle. Which one have you fallen in love with?"

"A man could do worse either way, but I'm not shopping for a wife. They've got something to hide or they wouldn't have ganged up on me at the interview. If someone gets to them first it'll stay hidden."

"Just keep your focus. Multitasking is just another word for ADD. In my work the ability to concentrate on the matter at hand is worth more than all the precedents in Michigan and the United States."

"Should I stand up?"

She scowled, looking like a beefy Dutch Boy in her gray bob. "Don't make sport of the national anthem. I do what I do for love of this country. What about Joey's other women?"

"What other women? There were only three. By wiseguy standards he was a eunuch."

"I don't mean romantic interest." She turned and fired the computer back up. The keyboard clattered, she pumped the mouse—on a pad, I noticed, with the face of Eugene Debs screen-printed on it—then stabbed a finger at a key near the bottom and sat back to wait.

I didn't know what we were waiting for, but I took advantage of the intermission to close my eyes and give them a chance to smolder out. I was feeling better by the minute, physically. Having a hangover always gives you something nice to look forward to.

Apparently I'd dozed off. A rattle of paper alerted me to

the sheet she was holding under my nose, fresh from the printer.

"Lee Tan," she said. "One of Joey's women, if you can use that term to refer to his heroin connection. She's still in the area. Good luck prying information out of someone who once reported directly to Chairman Mao."

I looked at the boldface print, then folded the page and put it in my pocket. "It'll give me something to do till quitting time at Iona's Simple Solutions."

"Just don't forget who I'm paying you to spring."

FIFTEEN

The city of Canton had started out as a commercial strip at the intersection of Ford Road and Canton Center—its original name, before it came down with delusions of Ohio—and grown every direction but up. Its newest focal point is a shelving and furniture store headquartered in Stockholm that attracts people from all over with too much stuff and nowhere to put it. You drive for country blocks and just when you think you've put the malls behind you and are approaching downtown you cross the line into Westland, and then it's more of the same all the way to Dearborn.

I thought it was a strange place for an international drug dealer to set up shop; but then the market is no longer just in places like Detroit.

Yesterday's storm had sponged most of the humidity from the atmosphere. Impressionistic strokes of cloud stood stock-still twenty thousand feet up, the bank thermometers read in the low eighties, and it felt good to hang my elbow out the window without grilling my arm on the sill. The gale had passed several miles to the north, leaving the petals on flowers growing in geometric shapes on rounded berms where the occasional landscaper mounted on a midget brush hog was cutting grass. When the wind blew across the slip-stream it filled the car with the smell of fresh clippings.

The address Lucille had harvested from the Internet belonged to a yellow brick building with tinted windows in a professional campus on Cherry Hill Road, a block south of Ford. White letters etched on the glass announced:

LEE TAN
LICENSED PHYSICAL THERAPIST

It didn't look promising.

On the other side of an air lock bounded by tinted-glass doors, patients and whatnot sat in upholstered chairs with bentwood birch frames, reading crisp magazines or staring off into space. There was the usual receptionist's counter with a sliding glass partition pushed to the side, and behind it a pair of women in casual but company dress, one on the telephone, dark and elegant-looking with a lilting island accent, the other making whispery noises on a computer keyboard. This one, chunky, with short-cut red hair like a copper bowl and a friendly face, turned from the screen to smile up at me. "Sign in, please. Is this your first visit?"

I must have looked worse than I thought. "I don't have an appointment. I'd like a minute of Ms. Tan's time."

"She's booked all day. Are you a salesman?" A little of the friendliness withdrew with the tide.

"I'm a detective." I showed her the county flasher with the ID flap folded back out of sight.

She paled a shade, and she'd had a redhead's complexion to begin with. "Is it urgent?"

I leaned an elbow on the counter and lowered my voice. "Not for the victim."

Lips pursed, she pushed back her chair, got up, and took the side exit down a corridor hung with photographs of happy people sailing and playing tennis: satisfied customers. In a minute she came back behind another woman and returned to her post. The woman on the telephone was interested now, although someone's voice was still spilling out of the carpicce.

"I'm Lee Tan. You're with the sheriff's department?"

I slipped that punch. "You're not the Lee Tan I want. Do you have a mother?"

"I did. Most people have had one at one time. Mine passed away."

"You don't know how sorry I am to hear that."

"Thank you." It lacked conviction, but then she seemed to have caught my meaning. She was a petite Chinese with features of polished ivory and an abundance of blue-black hair pinned back and falling behind her. She wore a white lab coat over gray sweats, gray sneakers with orange stripes, and carried a steel clipboard with several pages attached. She couldn't have been much more than thirty.

"Joey Ballista," I said. "Did your mother ever mention that name?"

Her eyes were deep mahogany. They moved to take in all the ears cocked in our direction from both sides of the counter. She made a little motion with her head and turned toward the back. I followed her down the corridor. From a comb behind her head her hair poured all the way to her waist, casting blue haloes under lights recessed in the ceiling.

We passed a room fitted out as a gymnasium behind a big window, where another woman in a white coat, younger than Lee Tan and occidental, stood holding an identical clipboard watching an old man in a white shirt and loose slacks picking his way between steel handrails. His eyes rested on his feet and determined lumps of muscle stood out like doorknobs on both sides of his jaw. Fists with pale knuckles tried to crush the rails.

We stopped inside a small windowless office done all in gray, where Lee Tan locked the door and turned to face me. An anatomical chart tacked to the wall showed a naked man with his skin peeled back to expose muscle and bone.

"May I?" She got rid of the clipboard and raised a hand toward my chin.

I nodded and she took it and turned the bruise her way. "Blow from a fist. I thought you detectives only came on the scene once the show's over."

"I got an early start." She had a firm grip and kept her nails short.

"Throbbing headache?"

"You hear it too?"

"Sit down."

I hesitated.

"No charge," she said. "Maybe you can fix a ticket for me sometime."

"That's not my department."

"I was kidding. I'm first-generation; we respect the law, even if we are lousy drivers. Sit down, really. I think I can relieve some of the pressure."

The room was only big enough for a metal desk and two chairs, an ergonomic item covered in gray leather mounted on a swivel and an upholstered bentwood that belonged to the set in the waiting room. I took that one and sat with spine straight while she circled behind me and took my head in both hands.

"You're with the sheriff's department?" she asked again.

"I didn't say that."

"Julie says you showed her a badge."

"It's discontinued. I use it to balance out my keys and change. I'm private."

"Insurance case? We get a lot of those: people suspected of pretending to have bad backs."

"Criminal."

"That's right, you said Ballista. I've heard the name. I read more than medical journals." She wobbled my head on my neck. I could feel the tendons relaxing. "Whom do you represent?"

"A lawyer is whom. She's representing Joey in a matter your mother may have known something about."

"What matter?"

"How much do you know about her relationship with Joey and his father?"

She stopped manipulating my head. I was in a vise. She leaned down and whispered in my ear.

"One quick wrench and you're a quadriplegic. Your call, but I wouldn't want someone else spoon-feeding me and wiping my ass for the rest of my life."

I reached for the revolver under my coat. She made a little movement, just a twitch, and both arms went dead. I couldn't have made a fist with a forklift truck.

"Oh," I said. "That much."

"Sensation will return in a moment. Stay still after that or I'll make it permanent. You told Julie there was a victim involved. Who?"

"There are two. A streetwalker named Frances Donella and an ex-cop named Randolph Severin. They both came to a no-good end."

"What's a private detective doing investigating murder?"

"They're cluttering up the job. It looks like I'm going to have to clear them up in order to finish it." Needles pricked my hands. The nerves were coming awake.

"What job?"

"Joey did a bit for attempted murder, back when you were twisting the heads off Ken dolls. Severin might have framed him. Donella might have helped him hang it. All I have to do is prove it. That means eliminating the women Joey had anything to do with as suspects."

She said nothing, going over what I'd said as if it were a patient's chart. The pressure of her hands was steady. The back of my head was touching her solar plexus. I could feel the measured beating of her heart, a plodding kettle drum against the rapid snare inside my own chest.

She gave my head an abrupt twist; I almost wet the seat, but then she let go and stepped back and I jumped to my feet and turned the .38 on her.

She had her hands in the pockets of her coat: concealed weapons. She asked me how my head was.

I rotated my neck without looking away from her. The thrumming was gone. She seemed to see that. "Whiplash injury, very common. It was a honey of a sucker punch. If

I were you I'd have an M.D. check for concussion. That's outside my field."

"If it weren't for concussions I wouldn't get any sleep at all. I didn't know your field included submission holds. Who taught you, the World Wrestling Federation?"

"I bluffed a little. I learned what to avoid, which is the same as a course in how to cripple a patient, but of course I've never tried it. Something inside would be bound to keep me from going that last thirty-second of an inch."

"You might have sneezed."

"It's a chance I was willing to take."

"I heard Asians set a high price on their ancestors. I didn't know it went so far as protecting the dead from legal embarrassment."

"My mother's name was Min. She and my father operated a meat market in Flatrock until someone herded them into the freezer and shot them for the cash register receipts when I was ten. I went to live in Detroit with my aunt after that. She raised me and paid for my education and training. She didn't want me dealing dope."

"You were named for your aunt?"

"She was the pride of the family: the most beautiful clothes, a big car, a swanky apartment in a building she owned. She bribed the Chinese officials to get my parents out from behind the Bamboo Curtain when they were newly-weds, put up their fare to the U.S., loaned my father the down payment on the store in Flatrock. She told them she was assistant to the minister in charge of the North American tour of the national table tennis team of the People's Republic of China. When they found out the truth, they considered her dead to the family. She didn't complain when my father stopped making payments on the loan, and not even when she was forced to assume the burden of my guardianship as my closest living relative. That was a biggie."

"Was I right about the Ken dolls?"

"It was worse. I had a vagina. The Chinese stopped throwing female children off cliffs decades ago, but the way many of them treat the ones they have no choice but to support can be almost as cruel. Crueler in some cases. Aunt Lee wasn't demonstrative in her affections, but I never knew anything less than respect from her, the respect of one human being for another, even when I did something disappointing, as I must have from time to time.

"I'm telling you all this because I believed you when you said you're working in Joey Ballista's best interest, not against it. If I hadn't—"

"I know. Gesundheit." I packed the revolver back on my hip. "Where can I find Aunt Lee?"

"I'll take you to her, but you'll have to leave the gun behind. Her instincts are sharp for her age."

"What age is that?"

"I'd say about the same as yours."

I thought that was pretty cruel, but there weren't any cliffs around to throw her off. I waited while she stepped into a room off the office and changed out of her working clothes.

SIXTEEN

She punched a button on her key tab, drawing a merry little puppy-dog response from a red Prius parked among real cars in a lot she shared with the other buildings on the campus. She'd changed into khaki slacks, a sleeveless navy top that showed the muscle tone in her upper arms, and leather flats.

I said, "I can follow you."

"No, you can't. I drive fast and I never look in the mirror. It's in the opposite direction you're going if you're headed back to Detroit. Save you some gas."

No one had lost me in traffic in years, but I had some more questions to ask, so I didn't argue. I snapped the Chief's Special into its compartment and locked up.

I'd barely strapped in when she took off like a quarterhorse on crank. We swung out onto Cherry Hill missing a minivan by an eyelash and got a boost from its horn accelerating to the speed limit. I dug my fingers out of the dash and turned my attention on her. She'd put on glasses with violet-shaded lenses in round white frames. Her profile was easier to look at than the road ahead. It was nice enough either way.

"She still dealing?" I asked.

"Not since before I graduated college. She got out when the Colombians moved in, before the floor fell out from under heroin. She saw the light."

"Born-again Christian?"

"Buddhist. It's a religion of peace. All the others only claim to be. There are no holy wars in its history."

"And no atheists in jail."

"It wasn't one of those deals. She never did a day, and she never used violence. The money came so fast everyone in the industry spent all his free time renting boxes and opening Swiss accounts. There was plenty to go around. As for morality, the poppy farmers back home had to live, and Detroit wanted what they had to sell. She kept the pipeline open."

"She poured poison through it."

"How many people died last year from tainted spinach? Honestly, who really cares if a movie star who makes twenty million per picture decides to spend some of it sticking juice in his veins? Not Hollywood. So long as he makes good at the box office, he can plot to assassinate the president and they'll re-up. Maybe give him gross points if he succeeds."

"She sounds like Mother Theresa."

"It was a rationale, and she rejected it in the end. She distanced herself from her past as far as is humanly possible: Gave everything to charity, the accounts in Switzerland and the Bahamas, the apartment house in Detroit, her cars, her clothes, the Americanness she'd acquired all those years. She speaks nothing but Mandarin Chinese, refuses even to pretend she understands English. I'll have to interpret anything that passes between you."

"That's a nice little ploy. Gives her more time to phrase answers to questions."

"Can you blame her? She spent every penny she had left on lawyers, fighting assault after assault by the State Department to deport her as an undesirable alien. Everything changed back home after Mao died. He helped finance the Communist Party through the drug trade, but once he was cold, everyone connected to him was declared open season. She'd have been beheaded thirty minutes after she stepped off the plane. It was Joe Balls who made sure the right people in Washington were paid off to prevent that. In Aunt Lee's thinking, her loyalty extends to him and all his seed."

"There had to have been something in it for him."

"Maybe he thought she'd be useful to him after she came to her senses. People who haven't found God tend to think those who have are going through some kind of phase. Then again, he might have found Him too. A lot of people thought he'd slipped off his rails toward the end. Madness and truth can be difficult to separate."

I was trying hard to focus on what she was saying. She made half a dozen traffic infractions while philosophizing. There are probably many Asian drivers who can operate dangerous machinery without a slip, but most of them seem to have stayed in Asia. I remember that drive against a score of blaring horns and screeching brakes.

"Did they ever catch the thugs who murdered your parents?"

"Never. I sleep nights thinking they screwed up on some other job and got what they had coming to them."

We broke a couple of other laws, then she reopened the line of conversation. "I know what you're thinking: Aunt Lee sent them to square the debt my father refused to repay. I sleep nights thinking she didn't. Revenge is a Western invention."

"So's the electric can opener, don't forget. Also iambic pentameter. I don't know how the world would've bumped along without it."

"I help people." Her hands gripping the wheel reminded me of the old man's on the handrails back at her office. "Every patient I send back to work or to play with his grandchildren helps make up for a junkie dead in some alley; that's how I repay her for her kindness to me. I don't remember my parents well. They seemed to have spent all their time cutting and weighing chops and steaks and adding up receipts at the end of the day. Aunt Lee always had time to take me shopping for clothes and school supplies and ask if I liked my teachers."

"Hitler loved his dog."

That seemed to have no effect on her. The Chinese aren't any more inscrutable than anyone else, and she was as American as I was. I'd had a bit to do with the children of criminals. They grew up in a world of judgment that sent some back into the family trade, others to their own personal Square One. Either course took up too much energy to waste in argument.

She pinked a light and bumped over a corner curb in silence, then: "Try not to mention murder when you talk to her. She'll fast the rest of the day to restore the balance, and she eats little enough as it is. I worry about her health."

"Can't do that, but I'll try to serve it up soft."

"Thank you." She shifted gears and subjects. "I notice you favor a leg. I hope you got it jumping off a lady's balcony."

"I stood in front of a plain old slug from a high-powered rifle. It went straight through muscle without nicking the femoral. You have to be good to do that."

"You were ambushed?"

"Not literally. I misjudged his mood. He made a more thorough job of it on himself after. It only gives me grief now when I do wind sprints. I didn't think it still showed."

"You're limping from habit more than pain. You should do more wind sprints."

"I try not to run unless someone's chasing mc."

"With a gun, no doubt. You sound like a private eye from the movies. I thought that was bogus."

"Most of us have enough material for a movie. The sequel's usually a disappointment."

"How about you?"

"I'm Freddy Krueger."

She laughed, a cosmopolitan mix of Yankee guffaw and Far East giggle. Her driving had settled down. She slowed for the yellow and surrendered right-of-way. "Sorry if I made you uncomfortable asking. It's the business I'm in. Most people, when they watch a football game, they see passes and intercepts and pileups and sacks. I see torn ligaments, compound fractures, herniated discs. My brain's a fluoroscope."

"I'm guessing your husband doesn't take you to rib joints often."

"He fell out of the practice, when I had a husband. I made more money, you see. He was a building contractor."

"He must've been honest."

"That's kind of a dirty crack, Mr. Walker."

"It's the business I'm in. When I watch a football game I see payoffs and adultery and dog-fighting in the off season."

"Are we flirting, by any chance?"

"I am. That dog-fighting line never fails."

"Seriously, now. I'm out of practice."

"You can say that again. Using an automobile for a siege engine doesn't exactly break the ice."

She laughed again. "Guilty. I might've made some progress if you hadn't distracted me into responsibility."

"If that was what I was after I'd have mashed down the brake from this side."

"What stopped you?"

"The console."

"I have a quirk," she said. "I like to test people, see how far I have to dig down to find the bigot. The progressives seem to crack first, oddly enough. How do you vote?"

"With a little yellow pencil. How far to your aunt's place?"

"Just a few more blocks, but it isn't her place. I told you she burned through her nest egg trying to keep her head on her shoulders."

"She's living with you?"

"Don't make it sound like I'm making some kind of sacrifice. She's good company, and I get to brush up on my mother's native tongue. A social life is just a substitute for family. Not much of a first date, is it?"

"Is that what this is?"

"You tell me. You're the one who brought up the subject of a hypothetical husband."

"I was flexing," I said. "I didn't much like that crack about my age. I'm just decrepit enough to take it personally."

She stopped in a school zone to let a female crossing guard shoo a gaggle of ambulatory backpacks across the street. "Some detective. I was batting my lashes."

SEVENTEEN

It was one of the older houses from the Canton Center days, re-sided recently with cedar and set in the center of a square of laser-trimmed lawn. A concrete driveway left a strip of grass between it and the house next door. At the end of it stood an old-fashioned one-car garage, unattached but with a covered dogtrot added on to provide shelter during the trip from car to house and vice versa. She parked in the driveway and we got out and entered through the front door.

The living room was small but comfortably furnished, with a chair and love seat covered in red nubby fabric, a Windsor rocker, and low tables for people to put their cups and glasses on. An antique French-finished wardrobe hid the obligatory electronics. Civilization is bashful about such things.

"Nice," I said, standing on wall-to-wall sisal.

"Not what you'd expect from a health-care professional with her own practice, you mean." She dropped her keys in a ceramic bowl on a table beside the door. "Between work and looking after Aunt Lee, I don't have a lot of time to collect trinkets and gadgets. Frankly I'm tired of places with glass shelves and ugly fertility statues and no dust. The woman who comes in twice a week has poor depth perception." She drew a finger across the surface of a table, leaving a track.

"What kind of looking after does Aunt Lee need?"

"She has no depth perception. Her ophthalmologists diagnosed her with macular degeneration ten years ago and prescribed eye drops, but she doesn't believe in them. Between you and me, they cost ninety dollars an ounce and she refused to pay it. Pushing narcotics doesn't come with a medical plan."

"She picked the wrong kind of drugs to deal."

"Snoop around as much as you like while I prepare her for your visit. She thinks INS, or whatever it's calling itself now, is sending spies to gather evidence to take another whack at her immigration status." She took off her sunglasses. "You're not, are you?"

"I'd have come here straight off if I was. They've got a better network."

"God help you if you're lying. She still has friends from the old days."

"I thought she was nonviolent."

"She is. They're not."

She went out through an arch while I put my hands in my pockets and took the tour. She had nice prints on the walls, abstract nudes with their skins still on, not like back at the office, a fistful of remotes in a miniature tin washtub on a table beside the recliner. The Zenith behind the wardrobe doors was a twenty-seven-inch tube, steadily going obsolete above a CD changer, a TV/VCR combo, bookshelf speakers, a collection of discs and VHS tapes that told me nothing about her beyond an interest in easy listening, action movies, and comedies. Art books on the coffee table, bestsellers and children's books in a knee-high case, all heavily browsed. It all looked like the package they gave you when you went into witness protection.

I liked it fine. Bland is comforting. Bland is safe. I'd had my fill of scarlet and black. Harry Potter and Meg Ryan make for a good place to bolt after a day of cops and cadavers.

"I gave away all my Nine Inch Nails after I got my MA," Lee Tan the Younger said behind me. "Patients don't react well to piercing and tattoos."

"I lost all my R-and-B in the divorce." I turned around.

She'd kicked off the flats and put on flip-flops, which for her appeared to be strictly house wear. It didn't take much off her height. She was tall for an Asian, if not especially so for a woman. Her chin came to my collarbone. She had pretty feet, with high arches and clear polish.

"Unfaithful?" she asked.

"Impossible to live with."

"All ex-husbands say that."

"I was talking about me."

She smiled without showing teeth. They were good teeth, too, what I'd seen of them, but she wasn't generous with them. I had the impression they were a gift she reserved for later. I'd had too much to do with what I'd had to do with to inspire complete trust at the gate.

"You go now," I said. "I didn't buy that 'I made more money' chestnut."

"It's a postlib face-saver. The real story's even less original: work two jobs to put someone through school, then when the diploma's on the wall and the offers come in, it's good-bye, baby."

"You called him baby?"

I only got to see the teeth when she laughed. "Bob, actually. You guessed right. He was a nice man, supportive, but dull as a putter, which was all he talked about when he wasn't talking about construction. He did well, but I didn't take a cent when we split, mostly because I'd treated him so badly. You don't accept anything at face value, do you?"

"You're the one married Bob the Builder."

"I got a lot of that. It didn't help matters." She seemed to remember where she was suddenly. "I suck as a hostess; not enough practice. I should offer you something. You're not a sundowner, are you?"

"It's dark in Alaska half the year. That can't be good on eskimo livers."

"I have a bottle of very good brandy, courtesy of a patient with a mortgage and just an HMO to keep him warm."

"He should dump the HMO and stock up on brandy."

"We have time. Lee's primping. She doesn't get many visitors." She crossed through the room to another arch beyond where stainless steel gleamed. "How do you take it?"

"Just as it comes."

She passed out of sight. Glass tinkled against glass. She came back carrying a pair of small snifters and handed me one. A swallow of honey-colored liquid lay on the bottom.

"You should've brought the bottle. You shook up my nerves back at the office."

"I said I was bluffing. Try sipping the stuff for once. It has a more beneficial effect when you let it do all the work. Good brandy is like hickory firewood, burns slower than poplar. You don't have to keep getting up and feeding the hearth."

"I don't have a fireplace." I took the recliner while she sat on the end of the love seat.

"The rocker's for show," she said. "Another tradeoff from a patient without a plan. I draw the line at livestock. Lee sits there sometimes when she's feeling matriarchal. She never rocks. That's character, don't you think?"

"That or motion sickness." I leaned sideways to clink glasses. "Just how many people did it take to put you through school? I count two so far."

"I was an awful leech. Lee was up to her neck in legal fees when I was studying for my master's. That's when Bob stepped in. He put in ten hours a day at construction sites. I couldn't bring myself to look into a part-time job with my courseload. I ought to have offered him a settlement later, but he'd have been insulted. Men are a lot more sensitive than women when it comes to money."

"You couldn't tell it by me. Nobody's ever insulted me that way."

She nipped at her brandy. I took a stab at mine. It went down on rollers and tingled at the back of my throat like hot peppers marinated in vanilla. "This is smooth stock. You must be a very good therapist."

"Van Gogh was a very good artist. He sold one painting in his life."

"Whoever bought it ought to have had a book written about him."

A voice called from the back of the house. The language sounded like someone plucking a guitar string.

Lee answered in the same tongue and put her glass down. "She's ready for us. She calls me child."

"Yeah, I noticed."

I finished my drink and got up and followed her. We passed photographs on walls, including a snapshot in a matted frame of a glum-faced Chinese couple standing in front of a low cinderblock building with a cow painted on the front. When the picture was taken it hadn't been the scene of a double murder yet.

At the end of the hallway she knocked on a door. Someone spoke on the other side and we entered a large bedroom that had been transported from the Forbidden Palace and dropped into metropolitan Detroit. A pagoda print papered the walls, colored silks hung from the rail of a red-lacquer bed piled high with pillows in satin cases, incense burned in the lap of a terra-cotta Buddha on a low stand with two cushions on the floor in front of it; one for the knees, the other for the forehead. The thin column of smoke gave off a gingery scent.

Two cane chairs and a sturdy club with embroidered arms completed the set, with a carved ivory footstool before the club to keep the woman who sat there from dangling her feet.

Aunt Lee was tiny and burnished-looking, all porcelain and enamel with hair as black as her niece's pinned flat to her head. She wore no makeup, but her brows were plucked as fine as silk thread and her lips curved gracefully. Her hands on the armrests were doll's hands with tiny perfect nails and nothing to indicate they'd ever been used. She wore a one-piece thing with wide sleeves and a long hem that glistened red, then gold when the light shifted. Paper slippers covered her feet. They might have been bound in infancy; but that was another generation entirely, and we were contemporaries.

Sitting there in no other light than what came filtering through pink blinds on the windows, she looked like a statue—the Dowager Empress in younger years, only not quite life size. She wore her niece's veiled smile. She was looking in our direction, but with the emptiness of eyes intended for display only. Knowing her troubles with the law I'd had my doubts about that part, but it wasn't a stall. Blindness is almost impossible to fake.

When Lee Tan closed the door her aunt turned her head a millimeter, but her eyes didn't move. Macular degeneration destroys frontal vision first, but I couldn't tell how much she saw from the periphery. I was suddenly glad I'd left the ordnance behind. She didn't look like the type that would grant a second interview if the first went bust.

Her niece said something in which I heard my name. Aunt Lee sat motionless until she stopped. Then she lowered her head, about half the distance she'd turned it to take me in.

It was an invitation. We took seats in the cane chairs, which weren't nearly as uncomfortable as concrete bleachers. We didn't cross our legs.

The older woman's voice was clear and youthful, well modulated so far as I could tell in the presence of a language that had stopped developing when Confucius was in short pants; had stopped because it had no more improvements to make. The niece translated.

"She wants to know if you have any connection with the police. I assured her you did not, but she wants to hear it from you."

"As little as possible. I'm not here to ask her about the details of the business she was in."

I waited through the exchange.

"She says she's glad, because she doesn't like to put people to the inconvenience of a long trip for nothing."

"She said it that way?"

"It's prettier in the original. She's invariably polite with strangers. The tradition is seldom observed today."

"Tell her our cultures aren't so different." I was pretty sure she'd understood the side conversation, but house rules are house rules.

From there it went this way, with the younger Lee interpreting:

"You speak for Joseph Michael Ballista?"

"I'm part of his defense team."

"I'll help as far as I am able. The incident you have come to discuss took place many years ago."

"I trust your memory better than Joey's. He isn't well."

"I am sorry to hear this, but I am not surprised. He was always"—the niece hesitated, searching for something suitable in English—"incautious in his habits. His father died of the same failing."

"Old Joe couldn't keep it in his pants. His son was better, but he wasn't any luckier with women. The case against him was constructed on evidence provided by an inside informant."

She greeted this with a twist of a beautifully molded lip, without waiting for the translation. She understood, all right.

"A woman," she said. "This too does not surprise me. Females are treacherous creatures." The niece turned my way. "The term is much stronger in the original. A vile oath, actually."

I nodded. " 'Bitch' doesn't go as far as it used to. Tell her it's the name of the informant I came for."

"I am not she."

"I made up my mind about that the moment I laid eyes on you. I was already pretty sure of it when your niece threatened to turn me into a vegetable just for asking about you."

The younger woman looked at me again. "I didn't tell her that part."

Smiling, the aunt spoke. The niece's cheeks stained red. It looked nice against the ivory. She responded in rapid Chinese. The language can be pretty, like raindrops on silver, or harsh, like strokes from a lash. In this case it was just flat. I couldn't tell if she was apologizing or defending herself. After a little pause the aunt spoke briefly in the same tone.

"Something?" I asked.

The niece shook her head. "It was private. Nothing of interest to you."

"Wrong. I'm curious as hell."

"It's one of those times I disappointed her."

"She didn't look disappointed. If I had to guess, I'd say she was telling you she didn't know you had it in you. She's just about the wickedest woman I ever met."

"I doubt that, Mr. Walker," Aunt Lee said. Her English carried a Midwestern accent. "You don't strike me as the wallflower type."

Young Lee Tan swallowed a gasp. I returned the aunt's gaze, directed at me from the glittering corner of one eye. "Was I right about the other?"

"You were close enough." So it was English now. "I knew Lee was loyal, but I could never tell how far her loyalty extended before today. It's reassuring to know someone else is looking out for one's best interests regardless of consequences."

"I'll take your word for it. I've narrowed the search for the snitch to three women including Joey's wife."

She shook her head slowly. "I never had the pleasure of meeting Mrs. Ballista. She wasn't present when we discussed business. I have to assume the same was true on the other occasions where his livelihood was involved. Sicilians have quaint notions about the women who share the marital bed. In that they are very like the men of the country of my birth, only without the open contempt."

"That was a different China," her niece said automatically. "The China of the emperors."

"Child, do not speak of things of which you know nothing."

I bore on. They could dissect history on their own time. "There was a girlfriend. She was sixteen when she took up with Joey. She did plenty of living in the meantime, but that came to an end night before last. The cops in River Rouge pulled her out of the drink yesterday morning."

I'd turned a little in my chair to watch both of them. Lee the Younger stiffened. I'd broken my promise to be gentle. Lee the Elder went on smiling. I was glad I was meeting her in retirement. In her prime she must have been like a warrior princess in a video game. "Her name?"

"Frances Elizabeth Donella."

She lapsed back into Chinese. Her niece stirred herself as if she'd been slow to listen. She asked a question, and when her aunt replied there was impatience in her voice for the first time.

I looked to the niece. She spoke without turning my way. "She said no, it was the one before who sat in on meetings. The English whore."

EIGHTEEN

Marcine Logan," I said.

Aunt Lee nodded without speaking.

"Why include her? She was sharing his bed too."

She held up a hand, stopping her niece in midtranslation. Once again she spoke in English. "She was assertive, that one, more intelligent than Joey, although perhaps not as wily as Joey's father, the one they called Joe Balls. Of course, she was quite young. She would be approaching her middle years now. I shouldn't want to do business with her without my young men from Hong Kong. I miss them the most. The majority of the world's population goes to its grave never having known a man who would die for them, let alone seven. Dead now, every last one, although only one for my sake. Three were slain during the gang wars in San Francisco. Tiananmen Square claimed the rest."

"Freedom fighters?"

"Fighters against freedom. The Shining Path never forgets an injury."

"Aunt Lee, you never told me there was so much blood-shed."

"I didn't think you could handle it, child. I've learned as much as any of us this day."

"Not to break up a tender moment," I said, "but why would Marcine throw in with the cops?"

"I don't know that she did, only that she must have had a clear understanding of Joey's affairs. I said she was intelli-gent. At that time, before they had Arab fanatics to occupy their days, the authorities were putting all their machinery behind the destruction of what they considered organized crime. I saw what was happening and slipped out under the wire. Any smart, ruthless woman would have done as I did. Marcine was both. I saw that on the acquaintance of sec-onds. But then unlike Joey I was observing her from the neck up." She sighed, a sibilant outtake of breath. "So many corpses at the bases of cliffs, and not one of them thought to apply the power they held between their legs."

Her niece's cheeks stained darker. "Aunt Lee, I've never heard you speak so."

The aunt went on as if she hadn't spoken. "How did the Donella woman meet her end?"

"She was garroted."

The smile turned down briefly.

"What?" I asked.

"Only that someone is trying very hard to assign this mur-der to the Combination. The current generation has refined its tactics and the last one to use the old is growing feeble."

"The same thought occurred to me." I stood. "Thank you for seeing me."

"Was I of assistance?"

"Actually, you made things worse. If Frances wasn't the snitch, I need another reason why someone put her in the river."

"You said she'd done a lot of living since Joey. If that means what I think it does, several solutions suggest themselves."

"The timing stinks for every one. Did you happen to know a Detroit Police detective named Randolph Severin?"

"I met a number of them on several occasions. It never seemed necessary to commit their names to memory. Was he with Narcotics?"

"Homicide. According to the department, Joey came close enough to put himself in Severin's wheelhouse. He's the one slapped the cuffs on him for dynamiting that reporter's car. The informant was his, but he wouldn't give me the name. I didn't really expect you to remember him. I'm just casting a wide loop."

Her niece rose, frowning. "I have to drive Mr. Walker back to his car. I won't be long. Do you need anything?"

"Just a few moments with my eyes closed." And she closed them as if we were no longer in the room.

Lee drove most of the way back to the office in silence, without committing any infractions. "You violated our agreement."

"I wanted to see her reaction when I dropped it in her lap."

"Did she pass?"

"I didn't expect any scenery-chewing. Do you know why *Candid Camera* went off the air?"

"I never saw the show. I heard about it. Kind of a reality program?"

"Yeah. We used to watch it to wind down from massacring Indians. The reason it went off the air is ordinary people stopped falling apart when they realized they'd been hoaxed. We all got too guarded after the rotten events of the Sixties. Reading people isn't as easy as it used to be."

"It wasn't easy containing myself. I didn't want to upset Aunt Lee."

"Her being so high-strung and all."

"Do you really think she's evil?"

"I said she was wicked. It isn't quite the same thing."

"That isn't what I asked."

"If there's a heaven I don't see her in it."

"She's never apologized for her past, but I know she's not capable of murder."

"Sure she is. We all are."

"Have you ever killed anyone?"

"I got out of Cambodia alive."

We cruised through another block. "What's a garrote?"

I told her.

"I thought it was something like that," she said. "I must have read it somewhere or seen it in a movie. She's right, you know, about the strength it would take. I've had patients who could barely walk but who fought like tigers when they thought I was hurting them. Hollywood makes strangling look too quick and easy."

"Getting it right would take too much time and film. Theaters survive on popcorn sales between shows. A bullet's so much more practical, like the one somebody put in Randolph Severin's head."

We were approaching a yellow light. She hit the brakes.

Another set screeched behind us. The driver leaned on his horn. She turned her head my direction. "You left out the graphic details before. Why spare her and not me?"

"You seemed okay with garroting, which seems worse. Anyway I'd already made up my mind she had no hand in that. I had Severin all wrapped up for Donella until that happened."

"What do the police say?"

"I'll have to get back to you on that. They'll have found him by now, but I don't know how long it will take before Detroit has it. It happened outside their jurisdiction."

"You *saw* it?"

"I came close. He was still warm when I got there."

"You didn't report it?"

"My civic spirit has some holes in it, especially when I've just shaken myself free of the cops."

The horn blasted again. She glanced up at the green light and we resumed moving. "How'd I do that time?"

"I wasn't testing. Sometimes you have to talk about a case with someone besides yourself and the police."

"I wish I believed you. I'm beginning to think I misjudged your character."

"I'm glad that didn't happen when you had me in your chair."

There were fewer cars in the part of the lot closest to the office, which had closed for lunch. I got out next to my Cutlass. When I turned back to thank her for the ride and the introduction she was already rolling.

I tamped out a cigarette and knocked it against the back of the pack, watching her swing out into the street without looking my way. When I lit up and ground the starter, Barbara Lynn came on the radio singing, "You'll Lose a Good Thing." Life's like that sometimes.

East of Dearborn the traffic picked up on the other side of the median. The afternoon rush hour started earlier all the time; it was only a question of months before it overlapped with the one in the morning, like baseball and hockey seasons. By the time I got to the Detroit city limits it couldn't have gotten any slower without going backward. A tractor-trailer lay on its side on the berm on the westbound where there was no curve or grade to explain it, a state police prowler had bagged a twofer farther on, a pair of vans probably speeding in tandem, and the usual innerspring mattress lay in the passing lane on that side, backing up the exodus all the way to Livernois. The smell of carrion had brought out helicopters from every radio and TV station in the area. It was a day like all the rest.

I picked up a prowler of my own ten blocks from the office, a Detroit unit. I eased up on the pedal even though I wasn't breaking the law any more than the next guy, but he stayed with me all the way without turning on his flasher or siren, and when I swung into the little lot where the attendant sat in his shack wearing the same clothes every day the prowler waited until I was in a slot, then stopped perpendicular to my trunk to block me from backing out.

I finished a cigarette and put it out in the tray while the uniform slid out from under the wheel, approached the driver's side between me and the panel truck parked next door, tapped on my window, and made a cranking motion with his free hand. The other rested on the butt of his sidearm in its holster.

"Mr. Walker?" He had one of those ageless freckled faces like Martin Milner in *Adam-12*. "I'm Officer Goetz. Inspector Alderdyce sends his compliments and asks if you can join him at headquarters."

NINETEEN

The female sergeant in charge of the little room where the servant met the public gave me a pass for the elevator and directed me to the second floor. She was medium brown with short hair bleached a defiant shade of yellow, built close to the ground on a wide frame. They don't recruit them off the runway.

Upstairs a sandy-looking party in his forties was sitting in one of the four hard chairs against the wall outside the office. He had a gunslinger's moustache with the ends dipped in nicotine and left his lanky legs stuck out in front of him when I approached, forcing me to walk around a pair of big-booted feet crossed at the ankles. He wore a beige uniform with an enameled shield pinned to the shirt and the hickory handle of a replica Frontier Colt in a holster leaning out from his hip. I figured he'd won it in a Tom Mix trivia contest.

"Hello, Homer," I said.

That made him raise his chin off his chest, but I didn't see his eyes until he slid his aviator's glasses down his veined nose for a better look. The mirrored lenses helped hide his bloodshot eyes from the world. "Do I know you?" His reedy tenor didn't go with the outfit.

"Save it until there's a witness present."

The slot next to the door had Lieutenant Hornet's name in white letters on black plastic. I didn't let it deter me. The occupants of two upper floors, John Alderdyce included, were bivouacing elsewhere until they were declared fit for occupancy. The historic old building was rotting from the top down, just like the city. I knocked and entered without waiting for an invitation.

An academy class picture of Hornet, thirty years younger and forty pounds lighter than the one I knew, hung on the wall beside a large-scale street map on a corkboard with tiny golf course flags pinpointing high-crime areas. From the look of it, locating the safer neighborhoods would have put far less strain on the office supplies.

"I'm mellowing," Alderdyce said. "Time was I'd have you pulled over, thrown on your face, cuffed, and perp-walked all the way up Beaubien."

"Thanks. I hate it when that happens."

I didn't take a seat, and he didn't offer to get up and clear the liquor carton off the only other chair in the ten-by-ten room. The box appeared to contain personal items, a bowling trophy and family photos in stand-up frames. The room was too small to share, so the lieutenant had been bumped, but the fact that its current occupant hadn't bothered to unpack or change the name beside the door was a vote of confidence in favor of the city's stalled plans for renovation.

"If you'd called me on my cell, I'd have driven myself

and saved the chief the price of gas." I leaned my back against the door and stuck my hands in my pockets.

"I tried six times. When was the last time you plugged it in to recharge?"

I took it from my pocket and tried my office number. Dead, like me. I was still waiting for the boom to come down. "I'm not used to it yet." I put the phone away.

"Where've you been all day? When you didn't answer at work or at home I sent someone both places."

"Canton."

"Michigan?"

"China." Which was almost true.

"What the hell's in Canton?"

"Why don't you just call in Marshal Dillon and get this over with?"

He made no move except to slide a thumb down the back of his tie. Today it was maroon on maroon, nearly as dark as his complexion. He'd imported his private filing system to the big yellow desk he was sitting behind: files and arrest reports stacked neatly in columns arranged according to subject. "After you put me on to the arresting officer in the Stackpole case I sent Hornet and a sergeant out to Portage Lake to talk to Severin. That character outside was already on the scene."

"Homer S Bruno," I said. "No period after the *S*."

"The surprises keep coming. I expected you to play dumb like usual."

"It got so I don't have to play it anymore."

He remained tilted back on his swivel, riffling the corner of a stack with a thumb. I didn't know who he was turning on the spit, me or the constable from Portage Lake. Finally he put both feet on the floor and got up and came around and pushed me aside to open the door and lean out. Something creaked, furniture or long loose bones, and the sandy-looking man in the uniform came in and slid down his shades for another glimpse. He gave it two beats to make my heart thump faster, then slid them back up.

"Nope."

"Sure?"

"Yup."

"Okay, thanks."

"That what you brung me clear out here for?"

"Yup."

He turned and strode out, creaking like a peg leg. The noise came from his gun belt; in addition to the big Colt, a pair of cuffs and a leather sap and a square Motorola the size of a gin bottle hung from it. A flat can made a circular bulge in his left hip pocket. I'd have been disappointed if it hadn't made an appearance.

Alderdyce swung the door shut. "It'll be a sad day when the last of those colorful characters retires."

"There's always comic books."

He went back to his swivel and returned it to its tilt. I transferred the liquor carton to the floor and took the hot seat. It was as hard as the ones outside looked. "What did he see?"

"Turns out he was at the marina when the storm was on its way, telling Severin he'd better close up till it passed. That's what the township pays him for, to tell people who've lived there for years what to do in heavy weather. Severin had a visitor. The description didn't fit you, but when do they ever fit anyone? I had to put the period on it.

That's what the city pays me for, to waste as many taxpayer dollars as possible."

"So it's your case now."

"We're assisting, because of the possible Detroit connection, same as with River Rouge. We don't get enough local murders to keep us busy." He slanted his big bony forehead toward the forest of flags on the street map.

"He didn't see the murderer. Anyone that handy with a forty-five would've done Homer, too, or scrubbed the operation."

"Sure, but it helps fix time of death. Thirty minutes from the first stumble of thunder to when the first witness showed up. The first official witness," he added, watching me with no expression.

"Ballistics said it was a forty-five?"

"Most like. Those unjacketed rounds the big-bore magnums fire would've done more damage to the window after Severin's skull got through with them. How much frisking did you do?"

"Just the blinds and his hands, to see if he slashed them up garroting Frances Donella." I watched him with plenty of expression on my face. I was still waiting for the blow.

"M.E. says the callosities make that part inconclusive."

"He said 'callosities?' "

"It's a word. I looked it up. It isn't like you to resist tossing a crime scene. Seems to me we've gone a few rounds over that in the past."

"I didn't have that kind of time. It's his busy season."

"Bruno and the county mounties got the call from a customer. Customer's sixty, one of those pillars of the community you read about in the obituaries. Severin was still warm when my team showed up. That's part of why I'm not all over you like boils on Job."

"What's the rest of the reason?"

"State can't afford to feed the prisoners it has, and it wouldn't do any good anyway. What took you out there so soon after our talk?"

"The M.E. said something about fishing line. I remembered Severin was monkeying with a big tangle of it all the time I was there."

"Thin as hell."

"What I thought, but I had to put the period on it. Did it turn up?"

He slid a sheet out of a stack and ran his eyes down it, put it back. "No tangle in the inventory, but our button-counters are still running it. Even a penny-ante store like Severin's puts a week into it after closing, to keep the governor happy. Couple of hundred miles of line on spools. Not enough to take him in and sweat him over, even if his glands were still working."

"Interesting if it's missing."

"Not to me. Maybe he got sick of wrestling with it and put it out with the trash."

"Maybe he threw it in the river with Frances. The current would've taken it miles from where the body bobbed up."

"You haven't told me yet why you like him for it."

"I thought if the Stackpole case was a frame and Severin couldn't be sure his snitch would back him up when it re-opened, he'd be out his pension and probably face jail time, even if the governor had to pardon a carjacker to feed him. He fit right into the box until that chunk of lead spoiled it." Something else I'd found out had done even more damage, but I didn't mention it. I was sorry I'd brought up Canton—the police file on Lee Tan would be at least as thorough as the one Lucille Lettermore had dug up, and cops could connect dots as well as anyone—but I have a policy of telling the truth on occasion. "Whoever fired it might have taken the fishline to implicate him, except he'd have dressed the scene to look like suicide. Trading one murder for another is fuzzy math."

"Maybe he didn't have that kind of time either, or maybe he's scared of thunder. The twerp in the morgue said it could've happened during the storm just as much as after. Did you keep your lights?"

"I did. A lot of people farther west weren't so lucky. It'd just passed when I got to the marina."

"Mine are still out at home, and I live only twenty blocks west of here. My wife gets testy when there's no hot water. Me, too. I break a lot of cases when I'm shaving."

I'd noticed he had more stubble than usual for that time of day. It was coming in pure white now. "It shows. What've you got against the M.E.?"

"He's a cocky little bastard ever since that TV show came on. We got a wall of photos downstairs of police officers slain in the line of duty and not one forensics expert, but if you watch television you'd think all the crimes that get solved get solved with egg scales and tweezers."

"That's what makes convictions."

"So does cornering suspects into tripping themselves up. That's a skill, too, and a damn hard one to learn. Some never do, and that's where we get police chiefs. God help us all when the pocket-protector brigade gets the green light to sit in on interrogations."

I watched him, fighting hard to play poker. I could almost see the first wisps of blue smoke from a full-scale burnout in progress. It made me sad. All the acquaintances of my tender years were bearing down hard on retirement, and all my investments were tied up in office supplies and ammunition. "Here's something else to think about next time you get to scrape your face," I said. "Severin had nervous hands. Most cops do; it's what puts some of them in hot water. If he wasn't working on that snarl of nylon, he had to have something to keep them busy when that door opened. But he was just sitting there with them empty when I found him."

"A gun, maybe. He had a case full of them and a chamois cloth damn near worn out in a drawer. Maybe he got one off first. I'm still waiting on a report on the carbon test we did on his hands. That's SOP."

"I didn't think to sniff them, but I doubt I could have told anything. I still smell charred powder from the store every time I breathe in. Anyway, I'm pretty sure the shooter never came more than a foot or two inside the door. Taking a gun out of Severin's hands would've been an afterthought. If he was enough of a pro to make a shot like that, he wasn't the type to second-guess himself. That bit about removing the tangled line was snatching at straws."

"Pros slip up too. We got a lot of 'em in Jackson."

I waited. Silence sagged and settled. "So am I still a suspect, or am I just up the same old creek for the price of my user minutes?"

"No to the first. I've seen you on the range. You couldn't hit a target at that distance with a forty-five if you threw it. As for the other—" He rummaged through one of his stacks, hauled out a file folder thick enough to strain the rubber band that held it shut, and stuck it out.

I took it and opened it. After shuffling through the dog-eared papers inside I said, "I guess it's too much to hope you're writing my biography."

"Unauthorized, if I were. There's enough here to bust your license six ways from Sunday if I sent it to state police headquarters in Lansing. Every obstruction of justice, breaking and entering, lying to the FBI—my favorite; you can tell tall tales to the cop on the beat every day for a year and we can't touch you, except maybe with a rubber hose—and tampering with evidence, all typed out with bullet points for the really salty stuff, the stuff that could put you in those shitty shoes they issue in the corrections system. Still got that unregistered Luger?"

"I'd answer that, but the Bill of Rights still had a couple of teeth in its head last time I looked."

"When was the last time you looked? Seems to me you used that piece a time or two. That's another six months right there."

"I didn't know you kept score."

"I've been a great one for keeping records ever since I did ninety days' desk duty for something a department commander told me to do. I've had this one in my desk for years; Hornet's, now, but you get my drift. Locked away. Not on computer. That'd be like putting it on a party line, and I like to keep the credit right here at home. There's a fresh crisp sheet on the bottom. I put it there not ten minutes before you knocked on my door."

"How far would I get if I tucked it under my arm and ran?"

"I'd put a slug in your good leg before you got a hand on the doorknob." He put out a palm, waggling his fingers. I laid it there. I'd seen him on the range too.

He opened a drawer, laid the fat folder inside, and locked it with a key he had on one of those gimmicks you attach to a belt. Then he folded his big hands on one of the stacks on the desk. "Run straight to me with whatever you dig up. Trip and fall down on the way and I'll show up at every parole hearing for the next ten years. Tough love, baby. The only kind you respond to."

I said, "Is that all you got?" But the *Edmund Fitzgerald* was sunk and I knew I was looking up at it from underneath.

TWENTY

'd been on the bottom plenty of times. I'd been in the hole nearly as many, but this was the first time I had to dig straight up from Australia to get a running leap. I fixed myself a dish of crow and knocked on Barry Stackpole's door.

Nothing stirred on the other side except a CD playing one of those mournful rock instrumentals that made a funeral dirge sound like the Ode to Joy. I knocked again, the earth made another revolution like a fat man turning over in bed, and a series of locks and chains moved two inches from where I'd raised my fist a third time. The door opened to reveal a Dorian Gray face with the cheeks still pink from the razor. His eyes were as alert and lidless as a bird's. When he saw who it was he took his head out of the gap and swung the door wide.

"I clipped you a good one," he said. "I guess I've still got it."

"You should've seen it a couple of days ago. Receiving visitors?"

He paused only a whisker. "Bar's open. Come in and gargle."

I walked around him and he closed up and worked the mechanisms back the other way. He had on a clean T-shirt and jeans; his writing uniform. He'd always said slacks were for writers who didn't write. They were no good for rubbing smut off a pencil eraser. The T-shirt was blank of advertising and clever repartee. I didn't think they made them anymore. Maybe he had them built to order.

He led me to his workroom, which had been the living room of the apartment back when a corpse had turned up in it; he'd hung on to the original sofa for horizontal thinking and ditched the rest to make room for a computer desk and related equipment, but hadn't done anything else to tailor it to his personality. Anyone who didn't know him might have thought it was a home office in transition toward becoming a living room. He'd stopped wandering, physically, but as to the creature comforts he might still have been living out of a suitcase for all the permanence the place represented.

The bar was a folding card table, with only thin lines of vinyl top showing between bottles and glasses and a faux brass ice bucket with cubes floating on top of the molten remains of their predecessors. He went that way, making no noise in stocking feet, and picked up a pair of tongs. He'd lived like the bachelor he was longer than most men had been married, but he was as fastidious as a spinster about certain things.

"Not on my account," I said, when he began forking ice into a rocks glass. "I'm riding the water wagon for a little, just to see what the Mormons are shouting about."

He shuddered a little, then dumped the cubes back into

the bucket. "I should've seen this coming when they strung lights at Wrigley Field. Next you're going to tell me they're breaking up the USSR."

"Don't teetotal just for me. I left my hatchet in my other suit."

"I haven't had a drop since I woke up with a sore hand and lost most of a morning wondering how come. When I remembered it scared the shit out of me. I'm sorry, Amos."

"Back at you. I ought to have waited until you were answering your phone before I started leaving my calling card all over town."

"Not an option. Lefty Lucy keeps a candle burning in front of a clock."

That made me think of Lee Tan and the perpetual flame she kept going in Buddha's lap, but I didn't want to get into that just yet. There was a patchwork Web site glowing on his monitor; I fixed on that, like the weather. "What's the assignment?"

"Nothing that pays, just doodling. Did you know Lucky Luciano took up knitting after he was deported? Woolen socks, to keep the troops warm at Bastogne. It makes you think."

"Nobody's all bad," I said. "Except maybe Air Supply."

He remembered the music then, found a slim gray remote among the barware, and switched off the stereo, a cheap Korean job on a steel utility shelf jammed with tattered books on the mob, the same collection of bound unpublished transcripts from FBI taps and flashy best sellers that had accompanied him all over the metropolitan area since Meyer Lansky's bar mitzvah. The room filled with the swish of traffic on Woodward, the only silence that downtown knew before the little intake of breath between the last factory whistle and the first crackle of small-arms fire after the bars closed at two A.M. He made a vague gesture toward the sofa and we slumped onto opposite ends. The cushion that separated us might as well have been the DMZ.

He read my mind. Everyone I'd spoken to lately seemed to have the gift. "I haven't had a flashback in better than a year. You?"

"I think about it, sometimes right in the middle of a conversation about something else. Not the same thing. It seems like something I saw in a movie."

"Shrinks I saw would call that part of the healing process."

"You saw shrinks?"

"Cable company I worked for answered to Hollywood; analysis was required, like morning calisthenics. Turned out I had issues."

"Had?"

"I got a clean bill of mental health when I quit the job. I only thought I'd lost bone and tissue. That charge blew away my identity, and I was using the camera and computer to find it. That elbow-patch gang has a sweet racket, like vending machines. You have to keep stocking up on candy bars and self-esteem."

"Don't go after 'em. They're all nuttier than Joe Balls."

He grinned then, that wolfish display of gums I hadn't seen in months. "I miss old Joe. He should've thrown away the kid and kept the afterbirth. So what do you think, did Joey do it?"

"You? I don't know. I almost forgot that's what I was hired to find out. Alderdyce pumped you on Frances

Donella. Did he get around to you yet on Randolph Severin?"

"You and I must've just missed each other downtown. I couldn't help him out. No witness to my whereabouts either time."

"He needs proof. I'm less picky. Where'd you go after you left my place?"

Putting it to him sober I didn't know what to expect. I pressed my spine deep into the sofa to brace for a looping right.

He didn't move a muscle, not counting the ones that lifted the corners of his lips. "I drove around for forty-five minutes, an hour. It's what you do in this town, because they let you. They don't cap you for speeding unless you mow down a troop of Brownies on a field trip to take in the Monets at the DIA. Then I stumbled upstairs to where we're sitting and drowned myself in a barrel of malmsey wine."

"Shakespeare, yet," I said. "Aren't we hell."

He went on smiling for an uncomfortable minute and a half, then suddenly tugged the white cotton glove off his shattered hand and turned both palms to the ceiling where I could see them. The stumps of his missing fingers had healed over without scars, pink as his palms; you wouldn't have known there was anything wrong with them if you couldn't count. There wasn't a cut to be seen. It comforted me as much as the prospect of peace in the Middle East.

I said, "I'll take that drink now, if the bar hasn't closed."

"Help yourself. Two fingers of bourbon for me, while you're up. I haven't slugged a close friend in close to forty-eight hours."

I found eight cubes worthy of the name, divided them between two glasses, filled them halfway, and tipped the bucket to top them off with water. I handed him one and sat down with the other. He frowned at his. "I'm drinking, not swimming. You used to pour it brown."

"Those two fingers looked kind of lonely at the bottom. Same old toast?" I lifted mine.

"I outgrew the custom." He drank, wrinkled his face. "You never know who you're drinking in this town. I taste a little Jimmy Hoffa in this one."

"They didn't throw him in the river. I think they built Ford Field on top of him. Speaking of bodies in rivers." I watched the wall opposite over the top of my glass.

"I talked to Frances a couple of times: once in Halston, once with more ladders than Engine Company Number Nine in her pantyhose. The wiseguys are harder on their women than the Taliban. She gave me zero both times, and she wasn't smart enough or dumb enough to clam up. She just didn't know anything. Whenever the conversation got interesting Joey sent her to her room to paint her toenails."

"Think she stayed?"

"She was working the counter at McDonald's when he found her. I damn sure do."

"What about Marcine Logan?"

He lifted his brows and lowered his glass to his lap. "You have been busy. Marcine and Frances weren't in the same league, and not even in the same sport. That English walnut doesn't crack."

"How many times you talk to her?"

"Once is plenty for running full tilt into a brick wall. It was before the big bang. I had two legs and all my digits and the blacks and Colombians were muscling in on the drug trade. When there's a war brewing, you go to the women for the inside track. She didn't even pretend to be dumb. She knew she couldn't pull off an act like that. She had her sights set on Joey long before they made contact; I found that out from her former friends. She only applied for that spokesmodel's job when she heard he never missed an auto show. If he got sick or had a contract out of town that week, she'd probably have had to settle for the CEO at Jaguar."

"Why not put in for CEO?"

"Too smart. It's the ones in the spotlight go down in flames when the heat's on—insider trading, falsifying stock-holders' reports, blowing up reporters. The ones who stand in the shadows move on to the next prospect. I came to the interview armed with all that, but all the leverage in the world is useless without an opening to insert it. She didn't cooperate."

I shook my head. "She only works as a suspect if she sold Joey out and did Frances to throw off suspicion when the case heated back up."

"She's no snitch. If she ever was even for a minute, it wouldn't have been for the usual reasons, money or fear of jail."

"Advancement?"

He nodded. "If something better than Joey came along."

"I don't guess that would be the receptionist's job at his wife's design firm."

"Jesus, you cover more ground than Hurricane Katrina. You talked to her?"

"To both of them. They Tweedledummed and Tweedledeed me square into a corner."

"Sure she's just the receptionist?"

"Silent partner, maybe. They're pretty tight considering the only thing they had in common."

"Silent partners put up seed money. The pawnshop value on chinchilla coats and jewelry wouldn't start up a Fotomat."

"Lee Tan told me Marcine sat in on all their meetings. What if she peddled what she'd heard to the Colombians and blacks?"

He looked at me. "Forget Katrina. You're global warming. How'd you track down that dragon lady?"

"Lefty Lucy. What do you think?"

"Timing's right. The new kids on the block shoved the old boys aside like tipping over a shithouse. They had the routes all down, made deals with distributors and customers in an end run around the Sicilians while they were busy raising the ante on their pet politicians to kill RICO in committee. Those old-school hoods never stood a chance. If Marcine was part of that, she'd have had bushels of case dough. Iona was hungry enough for success on her own to put aside a little thing like her prospective partner's screwing her husband."

I played with my drink. "I don't see either of them slipping a line over Frances' head and hauling back, or capping Severin with heavy artillery."

"A woman like Marcine would know who to recruit for both jobs. Iona's Simple Solutions is starting to draw some serious water. If for some reason Iona or Marcine saw that old mess of Joey's as a threat—" He flipped an ice cube into his mouth and crunched down.

"So they hung a label on Frances and took out Severin so he couldn't say she wasn't the snitch. That still leaves his murder flapping in the wind."

"Maybe she's not through."

TWENTY-ONE

heard Lee Tan got religion," Barry said. "Anything to it?"

I let that settle for a second. Changing subjects seemed to be the order of the day. "She dresses like Fu Manchu's daughter and keeps a statue of Buddha in her room. I don't know enough about it to weigh in on either side."

"Anyone can get the hardware. Pottery Barn's rotten with it. Madonna's gone Jewish. She ought to change her name, but she's got too much tied up in it."

"Crooks find God, pop stars go into rehab. It's the same side of the same dirty coin. The left-handed dollar."

"She's not all bad. Lee Tan, not Madonna; I saw her last video. In her time Lee was the Gandhi of poison-pushers. Not many of them come out without blood on their skirts. I can't think of even one apart from her."

"She makes good on her debts," I said. "Joe Balls pulled some strings on her behalf he might've saved for his own rainy day. Then he went and died and Joey Ballistic inherited his good turn." I rotated the glass between my palms.

I'd been watching the ice go back to its former life. "You remember John Hiller?"

"Tigers reliever, back before baseball went corporate. He had a bucket of strikes with no bottom. We talking sports now, or is this some kind of bullshit allegory? I thought that was my job."

"He had a heart bypass in his twenties. Before that he was a dependable pitcher, nothing more than that. You don't make the Hall of Fame just doing the job you were hired for. When he got out of recovery he lit up the top of every order in both leagues. When he got bored he'd throw three straight balls, then three strikes just for fun."

"I remember. So where's he now?"

"Cooperstown. What kind of reporter do you think you'd be if Joey or whoever hadn't made you Jack-in-the-Box?"

"What kind of detective would you be if you hadn't clocked a politician's son in the locker room at Thirteen Hundred?"

"The kind I am. John Alderdyce told me he missed a promotion because a commander forgot an order he gave him. He waited it out and took his turn when it came. Until he said that I'd never have pegged him for being less impatient than I am." I set my drink untasted on an end table. "Answering a question with a question isn't the same as answering it."

"I'd be right where I am, except I'd be walking on flesh and muscle instead of space-age plastic, and my headaches would be my own damn fault. Don't try to make Joey out to be some kind of collateral saint."

"What if it wasn't Joey?"

"I don't give a shit about Joey. If he went away for

something he didn't do, it would be for something he did do and the system didn't make the match. But I'd kill whoever did it."

"Seriously? Or is it some kind of bullshit allegory?"

He shook his head. "A life for a leg is antibiblical. The law expires short of murder like a winning lottery ticket, and I'm no good at demolitions, so I'd use the authority I have: I'd dig past him down to the first sign of root rot and bring it up to the surface till the stink got so bad he'll wish he finished the job."

"That's the guy I'm looking for," I said. "It never was about clearing Joey."

"Hell, Amos. I always knew that. Lettermore doesn't. I just didn't want you stirring up so much dust she'd throw it in some judge's eyes and make him a celebrity hero."

"She says she can clear him on DNA evidence if that wad of gum the dynamiter used to stick down the wires turns up. It's missing from the evidence room."

"Nothing sinister there. Attention to detail goes down exponentially with time. It probably fell out of a box when it was being moved to make room for a fresher case and somebody picked it up and threw it away. That, or it was misfiled. Carelessness blows more cases than simple corruption."

"If it was misfiled, she'll find it. She's a pit bull."

"If it lost its tag, she's still screwed. Chewing gum's a staple at most crime scenes."

"Let's not talk about gum anymore," I said. "Do you really think Marcine will go on killing till the cops run out of witnesses? It seems kind of sloppy."

"That's why I don't really make her for it. If she had

Frances done to keep her from denying she ratted out Joey, then slapped Severin into the corner pocket to keep him from fingering her, she'd have made sure the investigation stopped there. It isn't hard to dress a scene to look like suicide."

"That's what I thought. What if someone wanted to make it look like that's what Marcine was up to?"

His ice was water. He flipped it back, shook his head again. "That's one too many frames, if Joey's in one of them. What's the benefit? Whoever blew me up could write a book about it after all this time, do the talk-show circuit. There's no reason to cover up. I like Severin for Frances. Where was her pimp when he ate that slug?"

"The cops are covering that. They're not dumb."

"Some are."

I nodded. "You ought to get a load of the constable who found Severin." I gave him details then. He hadn't known I'd been on the scene at Portage Lake.

He whistled softly. "Alderdyce is slipping. In the old days you'd still be in Holding."

"He blackmailed me with my record. I'm his stringer now, an extra pair of eyes and legs free of charge to the citizenry."

"There's got to be more to it than that."

"I think so too. I did him a good turn a while back, or tried to. It didn't pan out and he wasn't supposed to know about it, but a favor's the same as bad-mouthing someone behind his back. Sooner or later he gets wind of it."

"Alderdyce was born downwind. I wouldn't depend on it when push comes to shove."

"Push always comes to shove," I said. "I have to deliver

if I'm going to keep doing business in this town. I'm used to that, but the older I get the slower I move, and juggling's a young man's game. I need backup. Can you find out if Marcine's got a hard interest in Iona Cuneo's design racket and vice versa? I need facts and figures, not drawing-room logic."

"So I'm your stringer."

"This one comes down to more than just a case of liquor."

"It always did, Amos. I can afford my own." He looked at my glass. "You didn't touch yours."

"I touched it."

"Fuck the leg. It impresses the hell out of women. I learned to live with the tin-skull headaches knowing Joey got nailed. All the aspirin in Walgreen's won't take the edge off until I can get back to that. I'll look into Marcine, to eliminate her as a suspect and settle my mind about Joey. They don't make a brand of whiskey as good as that."

I dropped by the office to slit circulars and charge the cell and check voice mail. I missed my old answering service, the husky female voices who'd gone to 900, but the recording I got was just as good.

"Mr. Walker, this is Lee Tan—the aunt, not the niece. I got your number from Information. Lee is out with friends, at my insistence. She thinks I think she works too hard. I may know something that will bring your investigation to a satisfactory conclusion. I pray I'm wrong."

TWENTY-TWO

The police report Lucille Lettermore had smuggled out for me was still burning a hole in my passenger's seat. I called her office number to see if she was in. There was a little hesitation after the fourth ring, and then her voice came on sounding as if she were shouting from Echo Point. I'd been transferred to her cell. She said she was on her way to meet a client and to slip the file through the mail slot in the door. Her building is an old one with some of the amenities still standing from a gentler age.

I caught a break when a car pulled out of a thirty-minute slot a few doors down from that pile and was getting out to feed the meter when I glanced up from habit toward her window. A set of pale green vertical louvers shielded it from afternoon sun. One of the blades shivered a little, as if someone had slid it aside to look out, then let it fall back.

It didn't have to mean anything, even though Lucille no longer had help to leave behind in the office. An ambitious cleaner may have seized upon her absence to get a jump on the evening; stranger things have been known to happen even in Detroit. The air conditioner might have kicked in, stirring the blinds with a puff from the blower. They might not have moved at all, and what I'd seen was an illusion created by heat waves from the sidewalk.

I was pretty sure it was one of those things, but I jacked in a coin just for the hell of it, lit a cigarette, and strolled down the street shaking out the match and flipping it into the gutter. Two cars from the corner sat a spotless gunmetal-gray Chrysler sedan with a government plate. The windows were tinted too deeply to see inside unless I cupped my hands around my eyes and leaned in close.

I didn't do that, and I didn't risk another glance at that window. Instead I kept up my pace, loitered around the corner to finish the cigarette, then retraced my steps and got into the Cutlass. I didn't start the motor. The city owed me twenty-two minutes. I rolled down the window for air.

Even then it didn't have to mean anything. Downtown is stinking with banks and other federal institutions. Inspectors and things are always running in and out. Lucille's building itself was still a bank despite a series of mergers, buyouts, and more name changes than Puff-Daddy-P-Diddy-plain-Diddy. But I was wasting Joey Ballistic's time, not mine.

For the next twelve minutes all the activity in the neighborhood confined itself to ground level. A black-and-gold city cruiser slid down the street on ball bearings and turned the corner, a flock of executive types crossed Cadillac Square on foot four abreast, two sweating in suit coats, one carrying his over his shoulder, leading the way with his paunch, a fourth in shirtsleeves and Tweety Bird suspenders and carrying nothing, the lad who used the company gym.

A seagull swooped at a candy wrapper cemented to the sidewalk. The cumbersome brown box of a UPS truck double-parked next to me. The driver climbed down in his brown uniform carrying a brown package, and went through a glass-and-nickel-plate door directly across the sidewalk.

That was par for the course. I sweated out five anxious minutes while he was inside, but then he came back out empty-handed, mounted to the driver's seat, and rolled off after taking a minute to rearrange some packages on the floor. The gray Chrysler hadn't moved. The meter next to it was flashing red. What'd he care? He worked for Washington.

Just as mine went red a stocky party wearing a blue suit too heavy for the season came out of Lucille's building, shot a glance back up the street and across, and made his way down the sidewalk with a little mincing step, carrying a pigskin briefcase. He blipped open the government car and slid in under the wheel.

Traffic was picking up. I reeled him out for a quarter block, then fell in behind and followed him all the way to the McNamara Federal Building, where he parked in a restricted slot and carried the briefcase up the front steps, moving at the same constipated pace. I found a place around the corner where the suckers parked and hiked back to where a row of identical gunmetal Chryslers stood against the curb. On the way I dialed Lucille's cell.

She was in her meeting, someplace with a tinkling piano and stemware shivering on metal trays. She listened to the short version, paused where under other circumstances she'd have inserted a "shit," and said she'd call me back in thirty seconds. Thirty seconds later she came on from a place where the ambient noises of the restaurant or cocktail bar were absent and demanded details. When I got to the pigskin briefcase she said, "Well, at least we can be grateful it wasn't a black bag."

"I think that's evening wear."

"The sons of bitches don't ever let up. Even atomic waste goes away eventually."

"Could be nothing," I said. "He could be a bank examiner. Some of them must look like J. Edgar Hoover. He even had the walk."

"I could be a U.S. attorney but it ain't likely. Where are you now?"

"I could strike a match on the Great Seal of the United States."

"Can you see his car?"

"I've got a visual."

"A visual, what the fuck's that?"

"I heard it on *24*."

"Never saw it. I work nights and weekends. Talk like a person."

"I can see it. It looks like part of a really dull parade."

"Whatever he took from my office, discs or paper, he'll make copies and put back the originals. That's how they work, so I don't know the stuff was ever missing. He knows where I am and how long I'll be gone; the bastards can tap telephone lines from their own desks now. I want you to be there when he comes back."

"I don't guess you keep an extra key under the mat."

"I can't afford to have an extra key. The guy who made it might make more. I thought all you private eyes knew how to pick locks."

"I thought all you lawyers stood up for the innocent."

"Never mind that. Find a wall to blend into or make like Spiderman and glue yourself to the ceiling and catch him before he puts the stuff back where he found it."

"And do what?"

"It's burglary. Use your instincts."

"Citizen's arrest?"

"Are you stupid? If you get busted I'll stand up for you, only don't get busted. Come back to me with what he took."

"What if it's got nothing to do with Joey?"

"It may not. My face is on more dartboards than the bull's-eye, but I'm no good to Joey if they suspend my license. Get moving."

After the connection broke I wondered if this was one of those things John Alderdyce expected me to report. I stopped thinking about it short of the answer and drove back.

There weren't any spaces left within six blocks of Lucille's, but that was okay because I needed cover. I put the car in a city garage, popped the trunk, and rummaged in the bag of tricks I keep under the false bottom until I found the little suede case where I carry my set of picks, a handful of plastic zip ties, the kind electricians use to bundle wires, and a heavy athletic sock. The last two items were street legal and easily explained to a suspicious cop, but the picks meant six months in the Wayne County Jail if I was careless, and another page for Alderdyce's file. I distributed the plunder among various pockets.

In the bank I handed a teller a ten-dollar bill and asked

her to change it into quarters. The skinny redhead said I must have a lot of calls to make. It was just my luck to draw a curious one. I told her I was going to have to break down someday and buy a cell. The motor-driven camera behind the cages made two full passes during the transaction, recording my features for the ages—or a week, depending on how often they recycled the tapes. I stuck the roll in my pocket.

There was another surveillance camera in the elevator, so I left it there for the time being. On Lucille's floor I scoped both ends of the quiet corridor for cameras. I saw none; there seemed to be one civil libertarian left in a position of authority. Maybe he was a cat burglar on the side. I went to work.

The picks were made in Belgium of case-hardened steel, but a tool is only as good as the laborer, and Lucille had a good lock. I stopped twice to let my arms hang and restore circulation, but at length the tumblers shifted with a little sliding whisper. No one came along all this time. Downtown looks busy, but the pedestrian traffic is scattered among a lot of buildings erected in the first flush of victory over the Kaiser. The elevator was just trundling down for its next load as I swept into the office and reset the lock. The car didn't come back to that floor. Breathing out, I leaned back against the door, broke open the roll of coins, poured them into the heavy sock, twisted it tight, and dropped it into a side pocket, breaking some distant tailor's heart in the process.

I left the lights off and took a turn around the room. After firing her last legal secretary, Lucille had pulled down the partition separating her private office from the reception area, creating a power center of space and sweep, with her desk and nerve-rattling collection of clocks at center back, a conversation area upholstered in leather dyed the color of ripe pears at front right, and a full bar enclosed in chromium and glass with a steel sink at front left. The carpet was an eye-watering green to match the walls, with an orange Greek-key pattern around the edge. I made shallow foot-prints walking across it that filled in by themselves before I could turn around to look at them. This center space was as empty as old Tiger Stadium and seemed nearly as big.

A gray scrim of sunlight through the shades softened the effect of the colors the tenant had chosen to shock confessions out of clients before getting down to the nuts and bolts of the wobbly system. To the left of the desk, the drawers belonging to a knee-high file cabinet—paneled alternately in green, orange, and yellow—were locked, but no one had improved on the standard bar mechanism since Clarence Darrow. The stocky fellow from the G would have sprung it in seconds and slid it back into place before he left. He'd have had less luck with the computer, although he'd have tried, until Lucille's fail-safe programs slapped his hands away from the keyboard. I didn't touch it. I'd never touched one yet, a condition of my contract with the Henry Ford Medical Center to inherit my brain when I was finished smoking it and pickling it in alcohol.

Clear Lucite frames on the wall above the cabinet held the lawyer's diplomas from Princeton and the University of Michigan, as well as certificates of completion of study at various self-defense institutions. She'd picked out her area of practice early, and had taken steps to secure her most precious commodity from assault. Some of these documents were recent; she didn't let anything slide. If ever an academy opened its doors to teach people how to avoid government spooks, she'd be the first to register.

As personal and professional spaces go—and in Lucille Lettermore's case they were one and the same—this one said as much about its occupant as a daily diary. She kept no journal, for obvious reasons, but the instruments you gather around you write firm and clear. I wondered if her spook of the moment had paused to take pictures as well as hard evidence.

I must have been wondering too hard, because at that moment something tinked at the door lock. I hadn't heard the elevator. He might have used the stairs, taking them with those baby steps. I crossed the carpet silently in six long strides and took up a post against the wall on the side where the door hinged, drawing the sock from my pocket and choking up on it so that the weighted end lay over on top of my fist like a jester's cap.

He was more efficient than I was, but he'd had practice with this lock: a clink, a rattle, a click. A pause to put away the picks, then the doorknob started rotating.

Once you know your heart isn't really beating loudly enough to give you away, you begin to perfect your timing. I waited until the door stood perpendicular to the wall and the man with the briefcase half turned to close it, then cocked my right arm above my head and tapped him ten dollars' worth on the mastoid bone behind his right ear. He dropped like GM stock.

TWENTY-THREE

He was a little guy, when all was said and done, J. Edgar to the life; insensate people often look smaller than when vertical, but the sloping shoulders and flabby chest that might have started out as muscle suggested a middle linebacker at least, at some school where athletics weren't all that important, and big men tend to walk mincingly more than shorties, with their Napoleonic strut. This one turned out to be five-six and a hundred seventy, if I was any judge.

First order of business was to check his vital signs. Coldcocking isn't an exact science, and without a medical history at hand I couldn't be sure how much damage a simple concussion might do to the system in general. The pulse in his neck was rapid, in keeping with a climb up an unairconditioned stairway in a suit he should have put away in a cedar closet until November. It began to slow as I held on, but after four minutes reached a level and remained there until I let go after another three. He smelled of some piney cologne mixed with sour sweat. Pudgy men in their early forties oughtn't to go about pretending to be Jason Bourne.

When I was sure he wasn't about to die on me I pulled his wrists behind his back, secured them with a zip tie, and just to put the fine point on it did the same with his ankles. Then came the detail work.

A thorough frisk job would require turning him over, but apart from the fact that he'd handle about as easily as a forty-pound bag of cement, I wanted him in a position where he couldn't get a good look at me when he came to, as people will at inopportune moments, and I didn't want to tap him again because I didn't know him well enough to dislike him enough to risk putting him in a coma. But I had all the time in the world, with a friendly location and a door freshly closed and locked against civilization, to search the obvious places.

He was Gerald Bertram Gull on the driver's license in his hip wallet, also in the picture ID in the cheap vinyl carrier he carried in his inside breast pocket, with a spring clothes-pin to hang on the outside pocket to get him through the federal building without being shot as a terrorist. He was with the Department of the U.S. Treasury. Not much help there. It's a catchall for investigation of counterfeiting, tax evasion, protecting the president, bank examination—I'd been close there, except the nearest bank was four stories below our feet—regulating firearms, busting moonshiners, and making sure private citizens didn't reuse postage stamps the cancellation machine had missed. I was pretty sure there was no still on the premises and that Lucille's postage meter would support the rent on the Capitol building in Washington. She didn't care too much for the current administration,

or any other since JFK's, but that situation changed every
four to eight years and she'd been in business for thirty. No
grassy knolls in her horoscope.

Gerald Bertram Gull started to groan. Knowing what
came next, I reached down, grabbed a fistful of his mouse-
colored hair, and lifted his head to allow him to vomit without drowning himself. When the convulsions were finished
I shook out a handkerchief with my free hand and spread it
as well as I could one-handed between his face and the
floor before lowering him back. He made a little sighing
noise like a contented baby and went back to sleep.

I dragged over his briefcase and examined it. It was expensive, with brass fittings and one of those combination
locks with milled wheels that work like a slot machine.
I took it over to the stainless-steel sink and walloped the
hell out of it until it sprang open on one side, grinning like
a drunken jack-o'-lantern. I made a mess of the utensils in
a drawer of the bar until I found a long-handled teaspoon
and made a mess of that prying up the other side. It was a
nice case, too; one more federal crime to lay on top of the
one that could put me in Milan until I drew Social Security.

He was a careful little guy. He'd had nothing more personal on him than his driver's license, not even a picture of
a wife or kids or a receipt from McDonald's to put on his
expense sheet, and his briefcase gave me only four CD's in
plastic cases with a jumble of letters and numerals written
on them in black marker, bound with one of those wide
rubber bands postal carriers use to keep their deliveries
from sliding all over the little Jeep. They looked like what
Lucille might be after. I got rid of the band and divided the

cases between my side pockets. I was starting to feel like Siamese kangaroos.

What to do with the carcass. Lucille wouldn't want him cluttering up her floor; the pool of onion rings was bad enough.

I got a grip on the zip tie binding his wrists, hauled him out into the corridor—checking first for witnesses—set the lock a third time, and pulled the door shut behind me, carrying the case. He was stirring again feebly when I rang for the elevator. I laid the case beside him and used my pocketknife to saw through the wrist tie, then boarded the car for the ground floor. I figured any man good enough to get around Lucille's lock would have no trouble with the zip tie on his ankles. The true test of character would be if he reported the incident to his supervisor.

Back behind the wheel of the Cutlass I hyperventilated into the heavy atmosphere, then tried Lucille. I couldn't get a signal in the garage. The attendant who took my ticket lamped me over like Joe Friday, but I didn't know him; it might have been his attitude in general. I paid him and drove several blocks until a red light gave me a chance to redial.

"What." No ambient noises now; she'd cut her meeting short. What had seemed like hours had been forty-five minutes at most.

"You need to tip your cleaning crew."

"I do my own cleaning. How bad is it?"

"Nothing mortal. The pay's not worth the risk." I gave her a guarded account of what had taken place in her office. I didn't trust the open airwaves any more than she did. She asked me to read off what was written on the CD cases.

The light had changed, but I drove with one hand on the wheel and fumbled one out.

"Where can we meet?"

"My office. I'm headed there now."

"Brother, that's me in your waiting room."

It was an exaggeration, but not by much. I took the top off the office bottle, inhaled the fumes, put it away, and was dumping out the sock on my desk when the buzzer told me I had a visitor.

She came straight into the rectory without waiting for an invitation. The color of choice today was tangerine, woven from some shimmery manmade fabric that changed shades with the light, with lime-colored slacks and a floppy *Working Girl* bow tie on a lemonade blouse. It was her idea of conservative dress for a first-time sit-down with a client, but it just made me crave fresh fruit. She looked squarer and solider than ever. Her gaze went to the pile of quarters. "Cash in an IRA?"

"Turning evidence into arcade ammunition." I got rid of the sock and started stacking the coins in neat columns like Scrooge. "I'm sorry about your carpet."

"Blood?"

"French onion soup, I think. I didn't look close. The B-and-E man's name is Gull. Federal ID."

"Never heard of him, but I suppose that's the point." She took in the rest of the room, which killed about a second; it isn't the Louvre. "Not online yet, I see. Isn't that taking stubborn just a little too far?"

"It wouldn't be stubborn if I didn't. I'm covered. I'm like the sailor who knows someone who owns a boat."

"Seen him lately?"

"Not since I assaulted an employee of the United States government." I pushed aside the stacks of alloy, took the plastic cases out of my side pockets, and slid them her way across the blotter.

She leaned a black portfolio case against the legs of the customer's chair, sat down, and shuffled through them, reading the markings and tipping open each one to look at the disc inside. Finally she drummed them together and put them in the portfolio.

"My client file, going back three years. I don't think it's the clients they're after, do you?"

"They'd need the military to run them all down, and the military's busy just now. How far out of shape have you bent the standards of ethics and conduct?"

"More than some, not as much as some others. They're more pliable than you think. My license was suspended once, but I represented myself and had it reinstated and the record expunged. I've been bugged, taped, followed, and photographed. A whispering campaign designed to muck up the jury pool backfired and got me a change of venue I sorely needed. Going black bag on me means they're determined to bust my practice for good."

"Jail time?"

She thought about that, shook her head. "Overkill. You can make a victim into a hero if you lean too hard. Look what they did to that creep Kevorkian. They had to have learned something from the way the whispering campaign turned out. It's a mistake to assume government is as stupid as its actions."

"I'd have thought Kevorkian would be just your kind of character to represent."

"I've defended sex perverts and traitors, but I draw the line at hypocrites. Call it murder, and I'm your girl." She shook her head again. "No, no jail time. The sons of bitches will be content to strip me of my credentials and back me into an on-air consulting position with some TV network. Draw my fangs."

"Is the Ballista file in there?"

"I said it went back three years."

"What's that do to our timetable?"

"Not a thing. If they put my practice on ice I'll second-chair some hungry attorney and run the show from there. He can collect from Joey and pay me as an advisor. You don't need Latin on a piece of paper for that."

"Like a coach still calling the shots after the ump throws him out."

She didn't react to that. Being a sports fan means having time to yourself. "All the same," she said, "it wouldn't hurt to pick up the pace. If the media moles in Justice let it leak that I'm a target, I'll be swimming upstream against paparazzi from here to Christmas. It could poison Joey's case by association."

"So it does affect the timetable."

"I talk around in circles sometimes. It's the job, get used to it. Anything new?"

"It looks like Marcine has more at stake in Iona Cuneo's enterprise than just a job in reception." I gave her what I'd gotten from my talk with Barry. I held back the call from Lee Tan. I wasn't sure why. The investigation seemed to have reached that stage where I plastered my cards to my vest.

"So you and Stackpole are back on."

"More like detente. He'll be harder to convince than a jury that it wasn't Joey who fixed that knock in his engine. Reasonable doubt won't be good enough."

"He was just the victim. I don't give a shit what he thinks." She shifted her gaze to Custer's Last Stand on the wall next to the desk. "I may have a line on that wandering piece of chewing gum. A load of evidence got packed home temporarily with personnel when the city evacuated those rotten floors at Thirteen Hundred. Not everything made it back into official hands."

"No good. You need to show chain of possession or they throw it out of court."

"Everybody's a lawyer since the Simpson verdict. Only they're not. The chain only has to be established by the prosecution. Evidence for the defense can be challenged, but the state has to prove it was tampered with to have it set aside."

"One wad looks pretty much like another. What do you say when someone asks if it wasn't just scraped off the bottom of a seat at the Fox Theater?"

Her eyeteeth showed when she smiled. For that reason she seldom smiled in court. "That's where the system screwed itself. Is that the police file?"

I had the folder on the desk. I tipped a hand toward it. She slid it her way, rummaged inside, and laid six black-and-white photos printed on grainy indestructible police-type stock next to one another on my side of the blotter. I'd seen them before: six different angles of what looked like a meteorite beaten all out of shape by its entry into earth's atmosphere, placed carefully in the center of a sheet of white paper to bring out the details. It was a good example of microphotography from back when the technique was still new.

"Bet you never noticed these were fresh prints," she said. "I had them made on the same kind of paper to reduce the chances of distortion and put the originals in a bank box before I let go of the file. When these were taken, DNA meant Don't Not Arrest. All the police cared about was preserving the bite marks to match to Joey's teeth. The dental expert they put on the stand helped slam the door on him. That was years before a judge reversed a conviction obtained on bite-mark evidence. It's discredited now. There isn't a DA in North America who'd touch it. But they had faith in it back then, so they committed every masticated sixteen-thousandth of an inch to the record."

"So if the real thing shows up—"

"When."

"—these pictures will identify it. Congratulations—if the DNA turns out not to be Joey's."

She stacked them together, returned them to the folder, and put the folder in her leather portfolio. "It will—won't? Whichever one is the one that springs him. It would be a very nice bonus if after we drop this bomb we can follow it up with another suspect. Put the screws to Marcine." She frowned suddenly, pointed an orange-nailed finger at the picture on the wall. "Why Custer?"

"Learning tool."

TWENTY-FOUR

After Lucille left I drew out the drawer with the bottle in it, then pushed it shut, went into the little water closet, filled the toothbrush glass with water, and drank it down in one smooth draft. I did it again, and you could still crumble my tissues and sprinkle them on a salad. I switched off the little dancing window fan and went home.

I slept the sleep of the sober. In the morning I retrieved my trousers freshly pressed from between mattress and box springs and broke a new shirt out of cellophane and put them on along with a snappy tie. I wanted to look respectable for my appointment in Canton.

The commute seemed shorter than it had the first time and probably was in terms of minutes. I never topped seventy but I passed a thousand cars heading east in the world's slowest conga line. It seemed the only people who didn't work in the city were the ones who lived there.

In the sprawl along Ford Road the shadows were shifting from front yard to back. The sun spangled off dew on the grass, then made a tractor beam that lifted it all in one piece, first solid gray, then growing transparent as it climbed, slicing into rainbows just before it vanished. It was worth getting up with the suburban stiffs to witness. I stopped behind a yellow school bus and watched it load from back to front at the entrance to a housing development still scarred with mounds of turned earth and fat tire tracks. The bus sucked shut its doors and fell into line behind two more collecting passengers along the same route. We had another baby boom going, only with quieter press this time.

Lee Tan the therapist's Prius wasn't in her driveway. My finger had barely touched the bell when the aunt called out from behind the house. I cut across the dogtrot under the canopy connecting the house to the little garage. The grass was damp in the shadows, chilling me through my socks. We go through three seasons every day in that climate.

The backyard was fenced in with tall planks of redwood, and a shock of color. Peonies grew in broad scarlet slashes through patches of poppies like orange crepe, lazy dusty-blue cornflowers, buttery marigolds just awakening, bushes so covered with living butterflies the insects appeared to be blossoming there directly, zags and borders and bowers and checkerboards made of primrose and daffodil and dwarf dogwood and flowers whose names I didn't know. Purple and silver tentacles in pots suspended from S-shaped staffs anchored in the earth spilled over the rims and hung nearly four feet to the ground. The garden of the Summer Palace in Peking must have looked something like it before the British burned it to the ground.

Flags of shale strung out like lily pads created a path into the center of the growth. I had to sweep aside a drooping branch of rhododendron, a feral-looking growth protecting the interior from intruders with thorns as long and sharp as the steel spurs the cockfighters in Mexicantown strapped onto their killers. The air was heavy with perfume and the brown, homely, not altogether unpleasant odor of fresh manure. A drunken bee wobbled from stamen to stamen humming an aria.

I found her humming also, kneeling over a bed of black loam with rows of yellow-green sprouts sticking up from it, aerating the soil with a pointed trowel. She wore a man's old dress shirt loose over snug black capri pants, crepe soles on her feet, and a straw hat with a low crown and a sloping brim that made her look like a coolie in *The Good Earth*. When she heard my footsteps she planted the trowel in the dirt with the handle standing up and sat back on her heels to shuck off her gloves. Outside the silken drapery of the bedchamber she was a trim, well-proportioned woman, and very small. She smiled at me, showing slightly yellowish teeth with sharp canines, and took off her sunglasses, the opaque black kind with hinged blinders on the sides. She didn't face me full on, but kept her head turned to bring me into focus from the edges of her eyes, dying as they were from the centers outward.

"Thank you for coming, Mr. Walker. How do you like my little time-waster?"

"I think they had something like it in Babylon."

"Buddhism is my faith, tending my garden my obsession. It's important I don't mix them up. I started with the poppies; such a beautiful flower, with so sinister a history. I'm surprised this country hasn't banned them. It outlawed hemp merely because it resembled its cousin, the marijuana plant."

"Hemp's not as pretty to look at. Did all this come from Asia?"

"With my reputation? Certainly not. Customs would have broken open the bulbs and scattered the seeds looking for raw opium. You're looking at an initial investment of ten dollars in seed packets and flats of bedding plants. Don't ask me how much I put into bringing them to the present pass. In the old days I was content to take my dividends in cash, but beauty is far more precious to me now. I shan't be able to enjoy it much longer."

"How much time do they give you?"

"To see? A year is optimistic. I get fierce pains every few weeks—agony, they are—Lee wraps tea bags in a damp cloth to draw them out and I lie in the dark waiting. Each episode accelerates the condition. I'd almost rather have the pain than the treatment. I'll have more than my share of darkness soon enough. Sleeping must be the same for someone who hasn't long to live." She showed those canines. "I suppose some would assign my situation to Karma, for my sins."

"It's hit-and-miss. A lot of people get sick and die who gave their lives to charity."

"Yes-s-s." She drew out the *s* as her eyes stole toward a limestone Buddha growing moss in the shadow of an enormous bougainvillaea. I'd never seen one so lush in that climate outside a greenhouse. "I besot myself with beauty, that I may draw upon it from memory. Am I pathetic?"

"I don't know. Ask Karma." I showed her the pack of cigarettes, then remembered. She carried herself so well you forgot even as you were discussing it. "Okay to smoke?"

"If you give me one. My ophthalmologists say no, but modern medicine is hardwired to condemn the habit regardless of the condition. It brings me repose, like burning incense."

I tapped one out two inches and came around from the side so she could see it and fork her fingers to accept it. I slid one into the groove in my lower lip and set fire to them both.

She drew an egg of smoke, blew it out her nostrils, and took the cigarette out to speak. "If the rude man who pokes at my nudity with instruments of glass and rubber can be believed, I shall live sightless as long as I saw, but I don't intend to withdraw into self-pity. There is music, and there are the sweet scents of this garden, and the taste of a rib eye cooked medium rare in sufficient fat to provide flavor. And of course there is sex. Do I alarm you with such frank talk?"

"Yeah. I thought Buddhists were vegetarians."

"Many are. But anything steamed makes me flatulent." She took one last drag and stuck the cigarette in the dirt. "You speak like a cynic, but your tone tells me you're just a disappointed idealist. I thought I saw a kindred spirit when we met."

"I tawt I taw a puddy-tat; but I was wrong."

She rose to her feet with none of the complaints of middle age. I offered her an arm, but she caught the movement and shook her head.

"I dislike being escorted. Lee suggested a guide dog, but in my culture they're considered unclean. I'd prefer a monkey. At the height of the Golden Age, the Chinese imperial court was a veritable primate house. The blood of emperors flows in my veins, did you know? On the wrong side of the sheet, of course."

I let her precede me along the flags. She was a tiny thing and a terrible tyrant.

"I'm not a monkey," I said. "Your uncle might be Genghis Khan, but he's deader than Frances Donella. On the phone I got the impression you had something fresh for me."

"The first sign of impatience you've shown. The roll of dynasties doesn't turn fast enough for you Yankee dogs." She picked her way along the uneven surface with care. "What I have to tell you is not for the open air of a garden. Lee and I have curious neighbors."

"I bet it's not because they live next door to an empress." I reached past her to draw open the door to a screened back porch, where she paused to remove her hat and hang it on a peg. It was a kind of mudroom with a pair of tired rubber boots lounging on a rubber mat and gardening tools of every kind hanging neatly in clamps on the siding.

She changed into a pair of paper slippers. She had beautiful feet like her niece's, but much smaller, smaller than my hands. A brightly colored silk robe with bell-shaped sleeves over her gardening outfit completed the transformation from field hand to royalty. Maybe her geneaologists hadn't been blowing smoke up her robe after all.

We went into a brushed-steel kitchen, where she lifted an electric teakettle off a counter. "Cheap tea bags are good enough for my eyes, but not my tongue," she said, filling a small plain porcelain cup with no handle. "Poor Lee has to drive all the way to Ann Arbor for my preferred brand. A specialty store there has it imported from Thailand."

"Not China?"

"Sadly, the land of my birth plants only rice where it cannot mine coal. The domestic product has fallen on the same hard times as your auto industry. Do you take tea?"

"Thanks, I'm not a fan."

The telephone rang. She replaced the kettle and scooped the receiver off a wall unit. After the "hello," her end of the conversation lapsed into Chinese. She switched back to English after she hung up. "Dear child. She worries me so. I think she's afraid I'll start a fire or wander out into traffic. She's coming home for lunch. We have an hour."

"How long have you been living with her?"

"Not long, but it feels like years. I never married. The glum arrangement between my brother and sister-in-law inured me against romantic expectations of the permanent sort. I fail to see how doubling one's misery makes it easier to carry."

"They cut you cold, Lee said."

"My grandfather exported opium to the Netherlands to finance a warlord during the twenties. I never knew if the warlord was a Republican or a Marxist, but a bandit is a bandit regardless of his affiliation. In any case our father, my brother's and mine, was too busy developing the North American drug market after the Long March to tutor us in family history. Later I employed professionals to provide details. Who is trustworthy, who is not? Often the answers lie in the tangled past. This is how I came to learn of my bastard ancestry."

"So you were born to the business."

"It went back five generations. My brother married a girl from a neighboring village and expressed his wish to live

with her in the United States. Any open criminal association would have denied them visas, so being an unmarried
female and therefore dispensable, I was indentured to serve
in the Black Trade, as we called it. The money was needed
to persuade immigration officials in both hemispheres to
cooperate."

"Your father must have intended to use your brother on
this end."

"Just so, but he died before the travel arrangements were
complete. It fell to me. A young woman's invisibility can
be helpful in avoiding a reputation for undesirable activity.
My visa came with no strings attached. You cannot help but
appreciate the irony."

"How much did your brother know?"

"He managed to display a great deal of surprise and out-
rage when I was arrested on suspicion of selling narcotics
in Detroit and my picture appeared in the papers."

She carried her cup into the living room and took her
place in the Windsor rocker. I sat in the armchair opposite.

"I paid for the happy couple's passage to America," she
said, "as a wedding gift. The loan I arranged to enable them
to buy the butcher shop in Flatrock was business. When
they stopped making payments, I realized they'd been
looking for some excuse to avoid their obligation."

"I don't suppose you took them to court."

"A person in my position didn't have the same choices
as everyone else. I was released for insufficient evidence,
but a suit would only have brought more unwanted attention. I wrote the loan off as a bad debt and deducted it from
my legitimate income. Lee told you what happened later?"

"She said her parents were killed during a robbery at the shop."

"One of those senseless things, and like so many of them, one that was never solved. I was questioned, naturally." She shook her head. "I wouldn't make my niece an orphan."

"I believe you. It doesn't matter because I'm not investigating just any old murder I come across. If you brought me out here to tell me all this, you're wasting gardening time. Your niece gave me most of it."

"I'm not a lonely blind woman desperate for company. The Black Trade kept my people from starvation through centuries of turbulence, but times have changed. I'd hoped by my retirement to close out a sinister chapter forever.

"It's Lee I called you about," she said. "I have an idea she's involved in the case you're investigating. It's possible she committed at least one of the murders."

I said, "I think I'll have some tea after all."

"Help yourself. The brandy is in the cupboard above the sink." She sipped from her cup.

TWENTY-FIVE

I found the bottle, a very good brand with a French label. The patient who gave it to Lee must have been satisfied with his treatment. Well, my jaw had stopped hurting since she'd made that adjustment in my neck.

I filled one of the child-size snifters. I wanted to drink, not just swirl and sniff, and I was pretty sure I'd be glad I had. This case was starting to have more suspects than clues.

Aunt Lee was enjoying her brew, holding the cup in both hands and sighing when she swallowed. I wondered if the stuff came with a hangover.

She seemed to sense my impression.

"The East gave tea to the West, among other native items, in return for the fruit of the poppy; but we retained the secret of how to grow it. Slave labor played its part. When I'm forced to drink the Western variety, I think freedom is overrated.

"I know I'm wasting valuable time," she said. "Forgive

me, but I rarely get a chance to speak of such things. Lee is a busy young woman."

"Busier than I thought, if your hunch is right. You said murders, plural. I only told you about one."

"She told me what happened to the man Severin. She didn't want to, but I knew she was holding back. I'm quite the bully in Mandarin, a sinuous language of which she is no mistress."

She set aside her cup. "I was gardening the other day when I heard the telephone ringing. Lee was out, so I thought she might have called to check on me. A storm had just come through and we had a power failure. Perhaps you remember it."

"I was in it."

"We got high winds, but no rain. I didn't want to alarm her by not calling back. She might think I was outside lying under a tree.

"I looked at the record on that receiver near you, to see if her office number had come up. I can see such things at close quarters. But it wasn't my niece who had called. You might have to go back a dozen or so to find it."

She wasn't going to lead me any closer, so I reached over and lifted the receiver off a slim telephone on a narrow table at the end of the loveseat, found the button that brought up the record of incoming calls, and scrolled back through unfamiliar names and numbers going back a couple of days. I was trigger-happy by the time one I recognized came up, and passed it. I thumbed back the other way. First the number appeared, then the name:

J. BALLISTA

She nodded when I looked up. "It sent me back many years. I thought it must have been for me, but I can't imagine where he got the number. And I thought it was significant that Lee never told me about it later. She always checks calls when she comes home."

The date and time confirmed what she'd said. Frances Donella's body had turned up only hours earlier. I thought of Lee's grip on my head when I sat in her chair. A garroting wouldn't be too much for a trained physical therapist of thirty or so.

"I found you," I said. "Through her. I surfed through all the Lee Tans in the book. Joey's network is better than mine."

"I didn't call him to ask. I thought perhaps Lee kept it from me to protect me from unhappy memories. You'll find no other such calls in the record. I checked."

She'd noticed I was still working the button. "Messages?"

"I played them back. The Joey I knew wasn't in the habit."

"I can ask him next time I see him. Maybe he just wanted to chew the fat with an old friend."

"I considered that. I even let myself accept it, until you told me of the threat Lee made against you in her office. She's very strong, isn't she?"

"A lot of people are capable of strangling a sick hooker. That line of work spreads motivation around like sexually transmitted disease. What would be Lee's?"

"If Joey feared the Donella woman's testimony might cost him his freedom, he might have called around among his old associates looking for help. They'd be more likely to recognize her on sight."

"You're a pacifist."

"A very unlikely suspect, which would be all to the good. And the favor I owe him is a very big one. Lee is very protective. If he threatened to expose something from our past association, I can't tell you how far she'd go to spare me."

I swallowed half my brandy and laid down the receiver. "These records only go back so far. You're suggesting he may have called before, got her instead, they came to an arrangement, and he called back to see how it went. If I took that back to my client I'd be laughed out of town. And I'd be laughing right along with them."

"As would I, if she hadn't offered to cripple you just for asking about me."

"Joey didn't know that. It hadn't happened yet. Pros hire pros."

"He's not well, you said. He may even have his father's complaint, which for reasons of delicacy we'll call lack of judgment. Lee can be reckless; you of all people know that. If it's a choice between her beloved aunt and a woman of the streets—"

"You're forgetting Randolph Severin. He was connected to Donella through Joey, and they died only hours apart. How well does Lee know her way around firearms?"

"I doubt she's ever held one in her life. When exactly was he killed?"

"The body was still warm when I found it, right after the same storm that put your lights out here."

"She came home early that day. The lights at the office were out, too, so she canceled the rest of her appointments. It couldn't have been much more than a half hour after Joey called. She noticed I was distracted. I told her thunderstorms upset me." Her canines showed, not in a smile. "I thought I was protecting *her*."

"That clears her of Severin, if you're right about the time. She couldn't have made it here from Portage Lake that fast. An hour would be pushing it."

"Maybe Joey made another call."

"Joey's been busy for someone in an ankle bracelet."

"Maybe it's time you paid him another visit."

"Maybe it is."

"Paid who a visit?" This was a new voice, although one I recognized.

Lee Tan, the niece, stood in the doorway holding her keys. Today she wore a short-sleeved top and a wraparound skirt that caught her just above a pair of round polished knees. She wore her hair as before, hanging down long and straight and midnight black behind her back. A frown creased her forehead. That hybrid she used for transportation was quiet. Neither one of us had heard her driving up.

I put down my glass and stood. I didn't know how much she'd overheard. "Joey Ballistic. I came by for some follow-up. Your aunt's the only one who knew him in the old days who isn't afraid to talk shop."

"You should've called me first. I didn't move her in here to make her sit through the third-degree."

"I'm a grown woman, child. You've forgotten I've sat through the real thing." She picked up her teacup, calm as Buddha. "I suspect Mr. Walker hoped to get a glimpse of you during his visit."

"So now we're in high school. Did you ask her to ask me if I like you?" Lee was looking at me.

"I'm guessing the answer's no."

Her keys crashed into the ceramic bowl. "Is my aunt a murder suspect?"

"She has a theory about the Donella killing."

"You must be pretty desperate to come all this way to hear someone's cockeyed story."

"That's the kind I hear most of the time. Some of them are cockeyed enough to be true. This one's a corker."

"Mr. Walker, I beg you."

"She can take it. I've seen her drive. Your aunt's afraid you murdered Frances Donella."

That stopped her. White teeth showed in an open mouth.

"What do you think, Ms. Tan? Is that a guilty look?"

"I can't see well enough to tell."

"You're not missing much. It's usually the innocent ones who look most guilty."

"And?"

"Search me. It's something I heard a cop say once. Joey Ballistic's number on your caller ID," I told Lee. "It showed up there the day the cops found her."

She went white as porcelain. "I—I thought—"

"That's a guilty look, I'm sure about that," I told the aunt. "If you people ever talked to each other, you wouldn't have to run around protecting each other all the time. Aunt Lee's version makes more sense than yours. You're the one with the guns." I'd closed the distance as I spoke. I reached out and squeezed one of her biceps.

"Oh, God. I was so—and I almost—My God." Her body went slack all over then. I got a grip on the other arm, but she didn't really need holding up. They only faint in novels. She shook loose and stared at me. "So why didn't I do it?"

"Because I know who did. I've known since yesterday."

TWENTY-SIX

Can't you tell me?" Lee asked.

"Not without proof. I hate being wrong in front of witnesses."

We were sitting in the front seat of my Cutlass, out of the heat in a spatter of shade from a maple whose branches trespassed on her air space from the lot next door. We'd said good-bye to her aunt and left her to her tea.

"May I have a puff?"

The Tans were surprising me today with their bad habits. You can always spot an amateur smoker. She had the gestures down but the smoke rolled out one side of her mouth while she was taking it in the other. She looked goofy doing it.

I said, "You must put away at least a pack a year."

"I've never spent a penny on one. Most of it would go stale. Sometimes when the walls close in I bum a butt off a pro."

" 'Bum a butt.' You must have cable." I took back the cigarette. It tasted of her lipstick, a pale pink shade. The moment was surprisingly intimate.

"Why don't you hand over what you know to the police? Gathering evidence is their job."

"You'd think, but that wouldn't clear the interest on my debt to them. I've got to unstep on a lot of toes to work in this town."

"Canton?"

"It's all Detroit to me."

"Keep your voice down. People here live their whole lives without ever setting foot in it."

"You could've said the same thing about me and Canton till yesterday, but now I'm an expert on the local floral and fauna. I need to tie this case up in bright paper with a Hallmark card or it's security work for me."

"And that's bad because—?"

"It looks pretty good from a hospital bed, but you can wind up there just as easily from a department store parking lot. I spent a lifetime in uniform in just six years."

"Which war?"

"Pick one. They've all been pretty much the same since the Bulge. I wasn't in on that," I added.

"What's the Bulge?"

"The Charge of the Light Brigade. Drop the bimbo act. They were still teaching history when you went to school. You're too young as it is."

"Too young for what?"

"Early retirement, and I'm too old for it. Stop distracting me."

"I didn't do anything."

"Didn't you? I thought you did." I got rid of the cigarette. The smoke clashed with whatever she'd put on when she changed out of her working clothes. She didn't use much but it had personality, the same chokecherry she used on her lips. Maybe not chokecherry, but it was how we met, sort of, so I locked it in.

"You're not so old. I was kidding before. Your hair isn't all gray."

"It's been not all gray since yours was in pigtails."

"Pigtails. Drop the codger act." She leaned in. She was all taut rope under silken skin and her lips were just as bittersweet in person.

When we finished kissing I used the headrest. "Joey had your number because someone gave it to him. If it was him who called. Anyone using his phone would've come up Joey."

"What will you do?"

"I asked Barry Stackpole to check out how deep Marcine Logan's involvement is in Iona Ballista's design shop. If she's a partner, she had to have had the money to buy in."

"Would the police pay her that much to inform on Joey?"

"It would depend on what the information was and how bad they wanted him. Busting up the Combination was high priority back then. If she had enough to persuade a judge to issue search warrants, it could be a tidy nest egg. Blowing up a reporter is a headline case. And giving Iona seed money to start her own business would go a long way to explain why she and Marcine are so tight."

"I can't fathom that. Not for money. If a woman was sleeping with my man I'd kill her."

"Not the man?"

"Too quick." She reached over and slid her hand behind my neck. Two fingers touched a bone at the base of the skull. "That's it, right there: the second cervical vertebra. It won't cure him of his fantasies, but he won't be in a position to act on them for the rest of his life."

"Do you always talk like this on a second date?"

She slid the hand around to the front of my neck, took my necktie below the knot, and pulled my face close. "Wait till you see what I do on the third." Her tongue flickered inside my mouth and she slipped out of the car.

Barry wasn't answering. I got the Repeat Dialing recording that meant his line was busy and cleared the signal without using the service. What I had to discuss with him wasn't for the public radio waves where scanners prowled.

I held on to that chokecherry scent as long as I could, then opened the window to cool myself in the slipstream. It had been a long time since the car had smelled of anything but private detective. The places the job took me were great for meeting women if you liked them dead or guilty of something.

Ninety-one, the guy said before I switched off the radio. Spirals of heat downtown turned the buildings into Jell-O molds. The pigeons perched on the ledges let their wings fall open to catch every little rumor of a breeze and all the pedestrians looked like they were walking uphill. My tire treads pulled away from the asphalt making little sucking noises like rubber cups; another day or two like that and it would be soft enough to swallow a mastodon.

I parked in the same garage I'd used the day before. I felt like a pot roast in a slow cooker. I couldn't wait to get out, and when I stepped into the sun-slammed street I couldn't wait to get back in. Inside the shelter of Barry's foyer the shade cooled me all over like a dash of water from a bucket.

He didn't open his door when I buzzed, but he was capable of ignoring all such interruptions when he was working. I decided to use the knocking pattern we'd come up with years ago to tell him who was calling. I hoped I remembered it right.

As it happened it didn't matter. The door was barely on the latch and drifted open an inch when I laid my knuckles against it.

The patch of sweat where my shirt stuck to my back turned into a sheet of ice.

Barry locked doors. When he didn't trust the lock he hooked a chair under the knob, and when he didn't trust the chair he shoved a piano up against it. He'd been off the endangered species list for years, but the habit of self-protection was grandfathered in, and Detroit was still Detroit. I fisted the Chief's Special and used the blunt barrel to nudge the door open farther, flattening against the wall to put eight inches of lath-and-plaster between my back and a bullet.

When the gap was wide enough to see part of the apartment from that angle I stopped. No shadows stirred. I heard only my own breathing, and when I stopped, my heart thudded between my ears without accompaniment. I let out my breath, took in a deep one, then spun on the ball of my right foot and used the other to kick the door all the way around on its hinges.

It didn't make it as far as the wall on the other side. Something stopped it in between and shoved it back as hard

as it had come. It caught me on the forearm and the revolver sprang from my hand and bounced off the opposite
wall of the corridor.

I dived for it, landing on my shoulder and turning onto
my back the instant my fingers closed around the butt. An
instant was too long. The door flew open again before I
could bring the gun around, but I bent up a knee in time to
trip the figure that came hurtling out. It fell headlong across
me with a surprised grunt, pinning my gun arm to my
chest, and before I could exert leverage to shove us apart,
an elbow caught me hard on the same spot where Barry had
connected with my jaw; a hundred years ago, that was, but
I was still chewing carefully on that side.

I didn't see stars. I saw supernovas. My vision went pur-
plish black, but just then the weight shifted away from my
arm and chest and I turned the barrel away from myself and
jerked the trigger. I felt the pulse of the report and the impact of the bullet at the same time, smelled scorched fabric
and cooked flesh and burnt powder. I felt the target shud-
der, heard it gasp, but it didn't collapse back onto me.
Adrenaline and shock prevented that.

Pinpoints of light pierced the black. It was like looking
through a sooty curtain. When the man—I was sure now it
was a man—scrambled to his feet, clutching his side, I saw
a narrow back in a hooded gray sweatshirt, shapeless legs
in droopy jeans three sizes too large, clodhopperish athletic
shoes pounding the carpet in the direction of the fire exit.
He bounded off both walls all the way and left a trail of
scarlet drops.

I took my time. I had it, he didn't, and I was still a little
too woozy from the blow to go haring off after a man who

might be armed as well as I was. I spent more of that time than I should have with the fire exit, but I'd come to distrust doors.

As it turned out I could have stopped for a beer. I found him on the next landing down, kneeling on the rubber mat clutching himself with both hands and staring at the floor.

I didn't feel like being Clara Barton. I had my equilibrium back, but my jaw was thumping like a basketball and I wasn't feeling too good about myself in general for the way I'd handled things. I put a heel against his exposed striped underpants and shoved him flat. He let out an animal howl and put his face on the floor. I moved my foot to press down on his spine, went down on one knee, and held the muzzle of the .38 against the base of his hood while I patted him down, avoiding the stain spreading from his shattered ribs. When I was pretty sure he wasn't carrying I holstered the revolver, jerked his hands behind his back, groped for and yanked out the drawstring of his hood, and tied his thumbs together tight enough to cut off the flow of blood. I tugged off his baggy drawers and used them to hog-tie his ankles to his hands. I had enough material left over to rope a calf.

He had skinny white legs peppered with pimples and what might have been old needle tracks in the backs of his knees. They were almost completely healed. Either he'd taken the cure or was so far gone he didn't care if the whole world knew his problem when he wore short sleeves. It was too hot for hooded sweats, but they're useful for confounding security cameras. So far I hadn't seen his face, but that could wait. It was close and sweaty in that stairwell and I was worried about Barry.

He heard me starting back up the stairs. A hollow, hopeless voice carried up the well. "Mister, please don't let me die in this place."

"You picked it." I kept going.

I heard the first siren starting up in front of 1300. The building was only three minutes away, and someone had reported hearing the shot. The workday was only half along, but Barry probably wasn't the only tenant in residence who worked at home. For once in that case I welcomed the sound.

He lay on his face across the threshold of his workroom in a T-shirt and chinos and the hard-toed shoes he always put on to answer the door. People have a bad habit of greeting strangers in their stocking feet, inviting a good sharp stomp with a heel and plunder to follow. But the precaution had bought him only a couple of minutes. Someone who knew his way around a blunt instrument had laid one behind his head, too close to the metal patch that replaced part of his skull for comfort.

I turned him over as gently as possible and found a pulse in the big artery on the side of his neck. I prised up his eyelids to compare the pupils. They didn't look as if they belonged to the same set. I'm an expert in diagnosing concussions from both sides.

I took a cushion from the sofa left over from the previous tenant and worked it behind the base of his skull clear of the pulpy spot and his shoulders to keep his lungs from filling with fluid. I smacked his cheeks a couple of times, as gently and firmly as possible, and got a groan. That was good; he could feel pain. I used the telephone at his workstation to order an ambulance, just in case the dispatcher who'd taken the earlier call hadn't done the obvious. When the casinos won't hire you to deal blackjack, there's always a job in public service.

His computer didn't tell me anything, but then they're always a blank wall where I'm concerned. I noticed he'd changed his screen saver from Warner Brothers Central Casting to a montage of real-life Prohibition goons standing around with their hats in front of their faces. He'd have shut down the system for safekeeping before he received his visitor.

The reason he'd opened his door to the kid dressed like Obi-Wan Kenobi lay exposed on the floor when I'd turned him over: a gray cardboard file jacket stenciled PROPERTY DPD—DO NOT REMOVE FROM BUILDING.

I picked it up and spread it open in my hands. Inside was a sheaf of green-bar computer printouts. The top sheet consisted of rows of six-digit numbers that didn't mean anything to me. I turned over the sheet and read the same numbers on the next page. Just to be certain, I thumbed through all the rest, all duplicates of the first. Barry would've known the file was a Trojan horse the second he turned the page, but the numbers printed there would've slowed him down just long enough for a kid dressed like an unofficial messenger to work his way behind him.

My toe struck something when I moved my foot. It rolled across the bare floor and stopped against the base of Barry's desk chair with a click. A cue ball's just as effective as a blackjack and you can carry it around in your pocket all day long without being arrested for it. He'd probably stopped in a pool hall on the way just long enough to swipe it off a table.

The siren was in the street now, winding down. I still didn't know the why of what had taken place and I couldn't count on Baggy Pants not to die of shock or loss of blood before he could make a statement.

I started with Barry's computer desk, and stopped there. Well, it made sense. The character with the cue ball wouldn't want to hang around long after the body fell, and the desk was only steps away. A shallow drawer built to contain a keyboard and small office supplies was just deep enough for the Colt .45 pistol that lay inside.

TWENTY-SEVEN

I hadn't seen Lieutenant Hornet in years, not since before he was promoted from sergeant and then shuttled off to hold the mayor's hand when he crossed the street. He'd been fat then, but the good life of shrimp puffs, bacon wraps, and strawberry mousse had turned him into a barn. He waddled back in from the hall carrying coffee in a silo and made a noise like a sail collapsing when he lowered himself onto the vinyl cushion next to mine. "Still here, I see."

I said nothing. I was handcuffed to the arm of the bench.

"You look beat. Sip?" He tilted the container my way. Coffee slopped to the floor. I'd moved my leg just in time.

"Not with that junk you dump in it. Don't all you cops have to have a physical once in a dog's life?"

"I got a drawer full of commendations and the department's understaffed. Also Hizzoner likes me. He was sorry when I transferred back to Homicide."

"I know how he felt." I asked him if there was any news on Barry.

"I didn't ask. Guy you shot's still in surgery. He's the one you should be worrying about. You don't go around shooting folks in the belly in this town. It's bad for tourism."

"Next time someone cracks open a friend's skull and clocks me one on the jaw I'll just ask for a restraining order."

"You didn't know about Stackpole when you pulled the trigger. I'm going to enjoy my job for once. Alderdyce'd be commanding a precinct by now if he didn't look the other way every time you wandered into a police case."

I let the conversation lapse. It was the same one we'd been having the last time we were together in a room, all those years ago. The room at present belonged to Detroit Receiving Hospital, where most of the shooting and serious assault victims in town go for treatment. I'd spent some time myself on the table there and was still paying down my last bill. A P.I.'s license doesn't come with a group health plan.

I was under arrest for questioning. The first officer on the scene in Barry's apartment had read me my rights and put me in holding while Barry and the character from the stairwell were being loaded into EMS units, or maybe one unit; there were a lot of official vehicles in the street by then and I didn't know what the policy was on separating assailants and assaultees since the price of gas went up. I'd cooled my heels there for a couple of hours until someone got around to a possible connection between the .45 in Barry's desk and the weapon used in a recent homicide with a suspected link to an old case in which he'd been involved. But instead of taking me to an interrogation room, the officers who checked me out had driven me in cuffs to the hospital and handed the key to Lieutenant Hornet in the lobby. It was unorthodox as hell and smacked of Inspector John Alderdyce.

Hornet was slurping the last of his coffee when Alderdyce entered the waiting room. The lieutenant had on a sport coat and size-fifty trousers that matched in some lights; the inspector wore a summerweight suit with functional buttons on the sleeves that hung on him the way clothes almost never do outside a magazine.

"Lose the goddamn bracelets," he told Hornet. "I told you he isn't a flight risk. You want to stampede all the visitors?"

"Regs." But the fat man leaned over on one ham and dug the key out of his pants pocket.

When he had them off I worked the blood back into my fingers.

Alderdyce told Hornet to go get a candy bar.

"I'm diabetic." He showed the inspector a fistful of Splenda packets from his coat pocket.

"I know."

He spread his feet and grunted and his face turned purple and he got up and trundled out carrying his coffee.

"You ought to assign him to the hospital full time," I said. "Save the department the cost of an ambulance."

"I've known him since his second chin. He used to be a good cop. Now he's just honest. I could wash him out on his fitness record, but he's only eight months away from his thirty. He can pilot a desk okay."

"He could be the desk. What about Barry?"

"Out of X-ray. Severe concussion, no fractures. That titanium plate or whatever it is may have helped deflect the blow. They're holding him a couple days for observation.

Your boy's more touch and go. That bullet knocked around inside him before it came to rest. Might have nicked the liver, they won't know till they track down all the fragments and reassemble the slug. That's how they do it, like the FAA and airplanes."

"Who is he?"

"Bobby Lee Jayson, Jayson with a *y*. His grandpappy came up from Kentucky to build Liberty ships for Old Man Henry, and that's about the last Jayson to hold down a job. Bobby's been in every precinct at least once, which is more than I can say for the chief. He's been busted for possession, using, home invasion, and aggravated assault. Did a two-year bit in Jackson for violating probation and entered the program. It didn't take. Pair of squad car officers picked him up with a rock of crack in his pocket last month. He's out on bail awaiting trial."

"You don't inject crack, you smoke it. I saw old tracks."

"The day you leave rehab, you go one of three directions: ahead, back, sideways. Bobby Lee took the third and traded habits. I'm surprised it took him this long to put himself back in trouble."

"Is it his MO to scam admittance in a home invasion?"

"No, he's an axe and baseball bat kind of guy, although the cue ball was a clever variation. There's nothing to prove that police folder had anything to do with the break-in and assault."

"Why would Barry keep a police file with nothing in it but gibberish?"

"He wouldn't. He knows our folders on sight, so it might have been enough to make him drop his guard. He ought to be locked up, the way he gets his information. We can't ask him what happened until he wakes up, and if Bobby Lee doesn't wake up we can't ask *him* anything at all. I'm considering adding today to your resumé." His tone was light, but it didn't extend to the brutal planes of his face.

"Sure, put it on my tab. I've only got one license."

A thickset man in Ford Motor Company coveralls came in, pawed through the magazines on the various end tables, and left, probably to buy a paper. It was all *Prevention* and pamphlets about what to expect after surgery. I asked Alderdyce what he'd gotten from the .45 Jayson had planted.

"*You* say." He opened a green leather notebook with gold corners. "Army Colt, military issue, model nineteen-eleven, fired recently. One shell short in the magazine."

"Prints?"

"Smeared. You hardly ever get a legible off a piece. We traced the serial number to the inventory on a batch of weapons stolen from a private collector in Harper Woods two years ago. Redford PD recovered most of them ten days later when they responded to a noise complaint at an apartment, ran a check on the party animals, found two outstanding warrants, and frisked the place on grounds of p.c. One of the suspects broke under questioning. It seems they were planning to use the guns to celebrate the anniversary of Columbine at a local school."

"Which school?"

"They couldn't agree on one. That's what they were yelling about when the neighbors called downtown. The oldest of them was only two years out of school. They all went different places and didn't exactly fill their yearbooks with autographs."

I couldn't decide if I remembered the case. Those things were beginning to run together like cheap summer reading.

"This piece"—he smacked the page with the back of his hand—"was the only one of the handguns that didn't turn up inside of a few months. They held on to the shotguns and full-auto rifles and sold or otherwise got rid of the hardware they had no use for, mostly without obtaining the proper social introductions. But guns have a way of bobbing back up to the surface in this town."

"Barry doesn't collect stolen guns."

"Only stolen police property."

"It was a cardboard folder. The Dumpster behind headquarters is full of them. What's the maximum on that?"

"He'll collect anything he needs to sell a story, and he's a paranoiac who's changed addresses more times than a floating crap game, to protect his skin. Where else would he keep a gun if not in the drawer of his computer desk? It's the only place he's ever stayed put long enough for someone to draw a bead on him."

"What was it doing in the drawer?"

He blinked. "I just explained that. I thought you were paying attention."

"You just explained why he'd have it in his hand when he answered the door, like any good paranoiac."

That made him quiet suddenly. The volume had been building until then and the silence rang.

"Why'd Bobby Lee knock Barry out if not to plant a gun that might have been involved in a killing he's already a suspect in?"

"We don't know that. The slug went into the lake and can't be compared with the weapon that fired it."

"What else would draw a homicide inspector to a case where nobody got killed?"

"That part may be just a question of time," he said. He was calm now. He always had been. His rages were generally staged to shortcut his way through interrogations. "I don't know much about computers, but the equipment Stackpole has lying around would buy a lot of crack and maybe a decent defense attorney when he goes to trial. Maybe it's our good luck Bobby Lee picked that address. Stackpole's got no alibi for either Frances Donella or Randolph Severin. Either one might have cleared the man he's convinced made him a cripple, and now we have a possible murder weapon in his possession."

"It's circumstantial. You said yourself you can't connect the gun to the Severin killing."

"I didn't say that. I knew you weren't paying attention. I said the slug wasn't recovered. Our team found a spent shell casing in a patch of grass outside the front door of the marina. The strike mark on the base didn't match the firing pin of the forty-five in Severin's display case, so we can rule it out as a practice round. Forensics agreed with you; the shooter probably fired from the doorway. We could use him on the range if he weren't a fucking cop killer."

I rapped the arm of my bench with a knuckle. "That's the other shoe dropping. I've been waiting for it ever since Severin. The murderer couldn't let the case hang there or the cops would never stop investigating. That's why the pistol didn't go into the lake right after the bullet."

"You can't make Bobby Lee for either kill. He can swing a cue ball hard enough—a little too hard for your version—but he's a druggie and way too shaky on his pins to handle a garrote with someone squirming on the other end. Plus he has no gun history, and between the eyes at that distance with a hand cannon takes beginner's luck to a new level. We'll set aside motive for now, which he ain't got, and dig into those would-be school shooters, but I'm telling you right now we won't hook up a gang of amateur terrorists with a garden-variety lowlife like Bobby Lee, so how'd he come to have the gun? Stackpole's the one with all the underworld contacts."

I glanced at the notebook in his hand. He was standing in front of my bench pointing a corner of it at me and if it had been a .45 I'd be dead where I sat. He saw what I was looking at and returned it to his inside breast pocket.

"No Bobby Lee," he said, "and I'll tell you why else. We ran down most of the people in Severin's address book. He wasn't the live wire in the group, but his relationships were mostly business, and he comes off as a square shooter on that account. Ten minutes before you found his corpse, he was on his cell phone ordering live bait from a wholesale supplier in Muskegon. He discontinued his landline when he got the cell because of all the storms out there bringing down wires. The supplier's caller ID confirmed the time. That morning, Bobby Lee kept an appointment in the City-County Building here with the public defender assigned to him in the possession case. The meeting broke up less than twenty minutes before Severin placed that order. Bobby Lee couldn't have made it to Portage Lake in time to pop anyone even if he had a car, which he sold to buy dope."

"He didn't have to be there at all. I didn't say he popped Severin or Donella. I knew you weren't listening. The only place he had to be is in Barry's apartment just before the pistol turned up. I saved him calling in an anonymous tip. He had the gun because someone gave it to him and told him to put it there."

He stood with his feet spread and his fists hanging at his sides: Rocky in his corner waiting for the round to open. I hoped he'd hit me someplace other than my jaw. It crunched like gravel when I wobbled it. "*Someone* doesn't cut it, Walker. Out with the name."

"Nope. A guess isn't evidence. A guess is my property and you can't have it. I'll tell you when you can. Did you get a record of any other calls Severin made from his cell?"

"We put in a request for a court order to get that from his server. So far we haven't found the phone. We figure the murderer took it for reasons of his own."

I felt like ducking then. It can't be safe having so many shoes hitting the ground all at once.

TWENTY-EIGHT

My cell rang while I was driving. Lucille Lettermore's number came up. I hadn't anything to report that couldn't keep, so I didn't answer. A couple of minutes later the gong went off that told me I had a message. It was Lucille, saying she hadn't heard from me since Pluto was a pup and what the fuck was going on, she had news herself to report. I turned off the phone. My news would stand up against hers whatever it was.

The sun had made its appearance, then drawn a dirty bedsheet between itself and the earth. The overcast offered no shelter from the heat, just screwed it down tight so it had no place to escape. When I rolled down the window the pressure from inside joined the pressure from outside with a blow that took my breath away.

I wasn't a fugitive from justice. Alderdyce had opened the coop, taking care to remind me just how short the leash I was on was; but I knew four blocks from the hospital just how short it really was.

I drove at a consistent speed. So did the powder-blue

Chevy strolling along a few car lengths back. In Detroit, where they let you drive, no two vehicles maintain the same rate of speed for long. The city was driving General Motors products that season, rotating as it did among the Big Three. This was an insult.

They were being stupid on purpose, and that made me careful. For sheer driving skill they don't come any better than the Motor City. But I was older and slower than most of the cops on the street and played dirtier.

The light was yellow as I drew along a row of orange-and-yellow construction cones sealing off an inside lane. I stopped, forcing the car stuck between me and my tail to chirp its brakes. When the light turned red I yanked the wheel hard to the right and hit the gas.

I knocked over half a dozen cones and wailed down the cross street a breath ahead of a city bus. Air brakes gasped, a horn lifted my shoulders to my ears—bracing for impact—but I found traction and laid down a plume of black smoke pulling away.

The Cutlass looks like a beater on purpose. The outside's a disguise, like a wig and a rubber nose. Underneath the dented hood and between the mismatched fenders the 455 is as clean as a cat's testicles. The tires are new and I get a tune-up every month even if it means I can't afford lunch.

I have luck, too; I had it that day. You don't depend on it, but you can't dismiss it out of hand. Whatever it was, blind chance or a drop in sugar, I left the plainclothes team staring at the stream of crosstown traffic and made a bracket turn west. Out in the neighborhoods I opened up the carburetor.

The ghost of Joseph Michael Ballista's mother hovered

somewhere above the private road bearing her name. It had been a sad life and short. I'd gone through a couple of incarnations myself since my last visit. The Elizabethan pile at the end of the limestone brooded under dirty cloud, the circle of lawn surrounding it as level as a crap table. The grass was trimmed and the windows sparkled, but it bore a sad air of neglect just the same. Where were the guards, the automatic weapons, the dogs that were part Doberman, part Stanley chain saw? There was nothing inside to protect. Joey hadn't put up much of a squawk when he found out Lucille had refused witness protection; he had nothing to deal. All the wiseguys had been trampling all over the code of silence so long no one had any secrets left worth killing to keep. It made you nostalgic for the old days of meat hooks and cement shoes.

I'd lost the registered .38 to the police pending investigation into the latest Detroit shooting. The holster was too small for the Luger, so I stuck it in my belt and put my coat on over it. It had no paperwork, but plenty of history.

The little plywood man on the grass wasn't sawing his log today. No air stirred this side of Canada. A bird started to sing, then ran out of breath. It reminded me I hadn't filled my feeder in days.

I introduced myself to the East Indian houseboy all over again. He gave no indication we'd met. Life at that address seemed to rewind itself to the beginning every time the door opened and closed. He let me into the naked foyer and went out to poll the master. His crepe soles made no noise at all, on a marble floor in an empty room. It was like a place in a dream.

In a season or so the boy returned—a boy wrinkled all

over like old vellum, his brown bare toes showing thick yellow nails in the openings in his slippers. It was an Oriental establishment in an English house with a Mediterranean resident. Very American.

"Mr. Joey will receive you, but he asks you to forgive him the informality of the circumstances."

"He's not naked, is he?"

"He is having a difficult morning. We are expecting his doctor at any time."

"A house call?"

"Dr. Nagler is a family friend. He treated Mr. Joey's father during his last days."

We passed through a series of echoing empty rooms like the looted chambers of a minor pharaoh, past the plush parlor where Joey had received Lucille and me the first day, and down a bare hall to a door the servant opened after one knock. The household seemed to be living on the ground floor exclusively. Climbing stairs would be torture for a man suffering from gout and everything that came with it.

"Mr. Walker." The houseboy withdrew, pulling the door shut behind him.

Joey Ballistic was sitting propped up in a big sleigh bed, one of the few pieces that would have been left over from the days when the house was filled with bric-a-brac from three continents, the lavish hoard of a first-generation father with the taste of a Sicilian goatherd. His cane leaned in a corner and he watched me with his dull dry eyes, hands twitching in his lap. The tops of his shoulders stuck up like staves under the green silk of his pajamas. "You don't remember me," he said.

"Sure I do, Joey. We met the other day."

"I mean before. I used to stock jukeboxes for the old man. We hired your old partner to ride shotgun, keep Jackie Acardo's boys from roughing me around and busting up the Sinatra records. Jesus, was you green."

So that was where he knew me from. He'd dropped right out of my head, a punk with a route. "I hear you had a bad morning."

"I had a rotten night. Try counting sheep when your heart's doing ninety. Gimme a slurp, will you? I'm spitting cotton."

A tall plastic container shared a bowlegged nightstand with glass and plastic bottles and droppers and a thermometer in a shot glass. The room smelled turpentiny with medicine. I handed him the container. It shook in both hands as he sucked on the straw.

"God, that's better than Blue Label." He gave it back. "I used to be a fair bowler. I almost joined the pro circuit. Now I can't lift a glass of water."

"Your old man wanted you to go into politics. You're a disappointment to everyone."

"Where's Lucy?" he said after a still moment. "You jump sides?"

"I'm still working your case. Couple things have come up."

"I know all about them fresh stiffs. Cops was here, but I had a character witness." He twitched a hand toward the electronic tether bulging under the covers.

"You haven't done your own killing in years. Frances Donella and Randolph Severin took you down once; that's the theory. They might've done it again."

"Fran didn't know nothing. She was just smart enough to

wiggle her ass when it counted. That's the only reason I kept her around. And if there's one thing the old man pounded into me it's never kill a cop, ever. That's like declaring open season on yourself."

The room's only window looked out on a triangle of lawn with a surveillance camera purring in an arc right and left. I figured it was a dummy, to discourage kids from scaling the fence and spraying dirty graffiti on the walls. I watched it make two passes.

He'd nailed the basic weakness in the frame someone had tried to put around him. Dopers killed cops, gangbangers killed cops, cops killed cops. The mob didn't. It was the only rival brotherhood Joey and his crowd feared. If one of them broke ranks, there would be no disclosure, no hearing, no motion to dismiss. John Alderdyce had once said there is no appeal from the court of instant retribution. If the cops didn't get to him first the mob would, for its own safety.

Well, I'd never really suspected Joey for Severin, with or without the tether nailing him down. A cop is a cop from the oath to the grave. Retirees count.

I didn't cut him loose, though. He was the only thing that tied Donella to Severin to Barry. None of it made sense without him.

None of it made sense anyway. I was dealing with a brain as loopy as old Joe Balls had been at the end, and Joe was dead.

"Maybe the killer wasn't sure about Frances," I said. "And maybe the cop killing was rigged to look like someone else did it. It would have to be, to clear you."

"If Severin said she sold me out, he lied. Why would

she? I was damn good to her: clothes, sparklers, a swell place with a view of Lake St. Clair, which I can tell you was a long way from cheap even then. I couldn't swing it now.

"Hell," he said, "it's less hassle staying home with the wife, even a bitch like Iona. But you can't show up at the K of C Hall without fresh pussy on your arm. You lose respect. I should of wrote her off as a business expense."

"Severin didn't name his snitch. He referred to whoever it was as a person. That's usually code for 'her,' so I made a tour of all your women. Your wife—"

"That bitch."

"Marcine Logan."

I couldn't read his reaction. He looked like a man watching his mother-in-law drive his new car off a cliff. "Mm. Marcy, let me tell you, you felt like a movie star when you stepped out with her. Photogs shot her more than me. She was ice, though, and *too* smart. At least with Fran I didn't think I had to read *Moby Dick* just to hold up my end of the conversation." His hands twitched.

"Lee Tan."

"Holy Christ. What's she up to these days? I heard the supply dried up when Hong Kong went Red. I don't see her working with A-rabs."

"Talk to her recently?"

"Hell, I wouldn't know where to start looking. What's the point? I ain't thought about her in years. Is she still even in the country? Seems to me she had some trouble with Immigration. The old man—"

"Your number came up on her caller ID."

"When?"

"Couple of days ago."

"Ojha!"

The houseboy came in. He had to have been listening at the door. I was starting to have some interest in him.

"Who used the phone?"

"Myself, sir. I called Dr. Nagler."

"Who else?"

"No one, sir."

"When's the last time you saw me make a call?"

"Weeks, sir. A month."

When Joey dismissed him I said, "He's on your payroll."

"I don't even like the things. My friends don't call or drop by, so the hell with them. It's just me and Ojha for company. He can't play euchre for shit, don't know his right bower from his left nut."

"How many extensions in the house?"

He thought. Those petrified-walnut eyes lost any resemblance to life when his brain turned inward. "Eight, including three upstairs, but no one goes up there but him, to sweep up cobwebs. He wouldn't call someone like Lee. He wasn't around when I knew her, and if you think I keep an address book you're dumber than Fran ever was."

"What about a phone card?"

"Oh, hell, seems to me I had one once, but I ain't used it all year. What good's it? I'm always home. Ask Ojha what he did with it. This sure seems like a mess of trouble over a broad I wouldn't know if I saw her on the street."

"I know. They all look alike." I saw her niece's face then. I was getting my fill of Joey. "Somebody tried to spray suspicion her way, to cloud up the investigation. That's just the kind of thing—"

Ojha, the houseboy, knocked and entered, as always without waiting for an answer. "Dr. Nagler, sir. Should I show him in?"

"Christ, I forgot." He looked at me. "We done?"

"Not quite. Where'd Marcine get the money to buy her way into your wife's interior design firm?"

"How the hell should I know? Maybe she sucked it out of Hank Ford's dick. She was working her way up from the floor at Cobo Hall when I found her."

But his head had started twitching, worse than his hands. It was catching. I shoved mine in my pockets to keep them still.

"I'm working a theory of my own," I said. "That she invested the money she got from the Detroit Police Department to rat you out in the Stackpole case."

"That's horseshit. I wasn't in on that, I told you. I thought you was in my camp."

"I wouldn't be if I didn't ask these questions. Start-up costs dough. You gave her clothes and stones and a crib, too, but they wouldn't go far in legitimate enterprise."

He looked at Ojha. "Go out and step on some hot coals."

"I'm not a Hindu." The houseboy's tone was as smooth as a dirk. But he left us.

"What do you need this for?" Joey said. "Lucy didn't send you."

"The case against you swings on how much Severin had to get the warrants he needed to hang you. I need to find the snitch and get her to change her story so Lucille can wash you in the blood of the lamb in front of a judge." I don't lie to people in sickbeds as a rule. But gangsters don't count.

"Shit." He rolled his head, pointed his chin, stretched

the wattles that hung like bunting from his slack jaw. He looked like an old tortoise fighting the temptation to withdraw into its shell. "She stole it, the cunt. Took it from the safe I used to keep upstairs. She must've seen me work the combination. Seed money I got from my partners for a thing I had planned."

"What thing?"

"None of your goddamn business, but they expected it back with interest. I was thin just then. I had to sell most of the furniture in the house to keep from paying it back with my hide. I took a bath, missed out on my thing, but it wasn't like I could declare Chapter Eleven. You ever see what a blowtorch does to a man?"

"Actually I have." I shook my head. "You're still thin. What's Marcine doing walking around?"

"I thought about it. Don't think I didn't. I was going through separation proceedings at the time. You been through a divorce?"

"Yeah. Don't knock the blowtorch."

"I couldn't hack it. Iona threatened to go public and name Marcine as a co-respondent. If Marcine turned up missing, I'd still be inside, and for all the wrong reasons." He put a hand to his heart as if to slow the galloping; drew a deep breath and let it out in a rattle that stood the hairs on the back of my neck. I thought about the doctor waiting outside.

"Well," he said then, "let her have it. She's the one has to deal with Iona. Hitting her would of been too quick."

I left him then.

I passed a tall man in the hall carrying a black alligator medical bag; I didn't know they made them anymore. He was thinning on top, in his sixties but fitter-looking than his patient by miles, wearing glasses with brushed-steel frames that matched his suit. He gave me a look of passing interest and kept walking. He'd have seen more interesting characters come and go in that house.

I found Ojha in a kitchen of polished granite and ceramic with a monster of an eight-burner stove designed for a hotel restaurant, probably a relic from Joe Ball's day, when gang wars came in seasons like hurricanes and street soldiers turned private homes into military barracks. The room was spotless, but the ghosts of ancient pasta and tomato sauce and anchovies haunted every corner. The garlic alone would stampede a colony of vampires.

He was smoking a cigarette near the range hood with the fan going to suck out the smoke. It was a pungent blend of Asian tobacco and smoldering dung. When he saw me he tossed the butt into a copper sink and ran water into it.

"Not on my account." I took out the pack of Winstons and shook one loose. One side of his upper lip lifted at the sight of the filter, but he took it, stuck it between his lips, turned on a gas burner, and leaned down to light it before I could come up with a match. I struck it on the edge of a counter and lit one for myself.

"We don't mention this to the doctor," he said. "I am a bad influence."

"Look who you're working for. Your boss told me to ask what you did with his phone card."

He ran smoke out his nostrils. "I have no personal calls to make. All my people are dead since Madame Gandhi. I am Sikh, you see."

"I thought you all wore beards and turbans."

"An animal is hunted for its skin."

"I'm rusty on my Kipling. All I want to know is what happened to his phone card. Whoever called Lee Tan could've left his number from anyplace, and if the card was used his number would've come up. I don't have to explain that," I added. "Your ear and Joey's door aren't exactly strangers."

"Are you suggesting I've overstepped the boundaries of my station?"

"You tell me. You're the only houseboy I've met since Agatha Christie."

"Houseboy; I dislike this term. I am forty-seven years old."

"Phone card."

He sucked in half the cigarette and laid it next to the burner to burn itself out. "I will show you."

I followed him into what had been the living room, where a handset rested in a formfitting standard on a bare maple floor. He bent, lifted the standard, and turned it bottomside up. A triangle of Scotch tape stood out against the dust.

"I placed it here," he said. "I am sure of this."

"Me, too. Who used this phone last?"

He thought, hard. When his brow cleared I knew what was coming. It was all I could do to pronounce the name before he did.

TWENTY-NINE

I was trying to get a number on my cell when the doctor emerged from Joey's bedroom. He had a pleasant, almost humorous face custom-built for bedside consultations. "You won't get a signal here; I've tried. Ask the houseboy if you can use the landline."

"Dr. Nagler?" I shook the hand he offered. "Amos Walker. I'm working for Mr. Ballista's lawyer. How is he?"

"I gave him something to slow his heartbeat. The body's a complex arrangement of self-contained units; when one organ perceives that the others aren't operating up to code, it goes into overdrive to compensate, regardless of the strain to itself. He should be in a hospital, but he says if he's going to be cooped up he'd rather it was here. He asked if I could recommend a good-looking nurse."

"I'm sure he put it that way."

"He's his father's son. Any more detail would fall under the category of doctor-patient confidence." He smiled.

"How well did you know old Joe?"

"He helped me pay my way through medical school after

my father died. My father lost his license to practice medicine for failure to report treatment of gunshot wounds. I suppose the loan was Joe's way of setting up a family health plan. I should add that I paid back every cent."

"Did you treat Joey's mother?"

He touched his glasses. "Did you say you're representing Joey legally?"

I gave him a card. "His lawyer's trying to get him a new trial on an old conviction. It's the first step toward getting that bracelet off his ankle. His mother died not long before he was tried the first time. If I can get a picture of what was going on then I'll know better what I'm dealing with."

"I couldn't do much for her. I recommended a therapist."

"Did she follow up on it?"

"No. She took her own life."

"Any idea why?"

He touched his glasses again. They looked fine as they were.

"She's dead," I said. "You can waive the oath. I won't quote you."

"It helps to have grown up in that atmosphere to understand it. Joe was old-school, and shielded her from the ugly part of his profession as far as possible. In return she shielded him by pretending ignorance. Then came the press: Someone wrote a series of articles about the Ballista family legacy, then others joined in. Try pretending to live a normal life when there are reporters in the trees surrounding your house with TV cameras and telephoto lenses."

"Joey was under arrest for planting a bomb in a reporter's car. They tend to take that kind of thing personally."

"You've mixed up the order of events. His mother swallowed a lethal dose of barbiturates weeks before that incident."

"I didn't know that," I said. "Her death didn't get as much play as the rest."

"I was able to help with that."

"You signed the death certificate?"

Glasses. "I cited cause of death as cardiac arrest, which it was. Everything else I told you is speculation based on evidence found at the scene. I broke no laws and violated no code of ethics, but I managed to keep a family tragedy from turning into a grotesque circus."

"I guess you figured you owed Joe Balls that much."

"I didn't owe him a thing except medical treatment when he asked for it. I'd repaid him by then." His voice was cold.

"Just the same, it was a long limb to climb out on if the authorities ordered an autopsy. Their interpretation of the law is less elastic."

"It was a question of human sympathy, not obligation. My father blew out his brains with a revolver when they took his license."

I got a signal six blocks from the house and returned Lucille's call.

"I haven't had lunch," I said when she answered. "I'll make a quick stop, then go over and talk to Iona Cuneo and Marcine Logan."

"What about?" Her voice gargled a little. We were both on cells.

"We were right. Marcine's a full partner."

"When did you find this out? Where are you?"

"Just now, and leaving Canton." I bent the light at Telegraph Road and turned north. I was only a dozen miles south of Iroquois Heights and Iona's Simple Solutions and a hell of a hike from Canton. "Lee Tan told me about Marcine. She found out Joey tried to call her recently; it spooked her, being retired from all that, and she made the decision to come clean."

"How did Lee Tan come to know about Marcine?"

This was trickier, not having had time to practice my stroke, but I took a deep breath and pushed off. "That *omerta* thing is a Mafia myth. They gossip like old ladies among themselves. Anyway it means I've found Severin's paid informant. The department must've really wanted Joey to shake loose that much case dough."

"What if she lied?"

"She had to have made it convincing. I'll ask her after lunch. I don't ask questions well on an empty stomach."

"After all these years? She'll just lie again."

"I'm used to it. So are the cops, and they've got plenty to lose if her testimony falls apart during Joey's new trial. They'll get the truth out of her if I don't."

"It doesn't make sense. If it's common gossip, how come we're only hearing about it now?"

"She doesn't have to know that's all it is."

"That didn't answer my question."

I should've taken more time to practice. She'd cross-examined experts. "You're starting to break up."

"Okay, we'll talk later. Anything else?"

I thought about Barry lying on the floor of his apartment, Bobby Lee Jayson trussed up and bleeding in the stairwell, the .45 that had probably killed Randolph Severin, the cell phone that had disappeared from Severin's marina, probably from his dead hand. He had to have been occupying himself with something when the bullet came; say, ringing off after ordering live bait from his supplier. I thought about what Ojha and Dr. Nagler had told me at Joey Ballista's house, about the missing phone card and Joey's mother's suicide.

"Nope. I'll report later." I hit End.

Next I called John Alderdyce's line at 1300. I argued with a woman and then a man, who transferred me to his cell. The whole world was rolling around jabbering like peas in an animated cartoon.

"I've been trying to get you for an hour," he said.

"I was at Joey Ballistic's. No signal there. I think it's all the antibugging equipment in the house."

"That where you went after you shook your police tail?"

"Yeah. You should've known me better than to try."

"Hornet's idea. I told him to go ahead and knock himself out. Anything to keep him busy. What'd you get from Joey?"

"Not much. He's under the weather. What's up?"

"Bobby Lee came out of the anesthetic, yelling for his lawyer. Guess what name he yelled."

"Lucille Lettermore."

The radio waves crackled. "You take all the fun out of guessing games."

"I stuck her at the top of my list when she tried to claim she was being investigated by the Justice Department instead of Treasury." I sketched out my brief encounter with Agent Gull. "She was a little too eager to find out if I'd had a chance to look at those discs he stole from her office in a computer. I didn't tell her I'd gotten a good look at Gull's ID."

"IRS?"

"She's won every round she ever had with Justice. It wouldn't be the first time a lawyer failed to report under-the-counter income on her ten-forty. She needs a big win in court to generate new business, enough to buy her way out of jail."

"That's a long way to shinny up a rope as loose as that."

"She hasn't had a high-profile case since Washington lost its interest in domestic terrorists. She can't afford to blow this one. Who represented those would-be school shooters?"

"Firm based in Toledo. No link there."

That took some helium out of my balloon. I needed Lucille to be the one who funneled the .45 they'd stolen from the collector in Harper Woods to Bobby Lee.

"How's Barry?" I asked.

"Resting comfortably, as they say. I'm at the hospital still, waiting to get in to see him. Where are you headed?"

"Tell you when I get there. Don't give up on those shooters. Those out-of-state attorneys usually consult with locals on the Michigan statutes."

"What've you got going, Walker?"

"I'm—" I tuned into my favorite all-static station on the radio, held the phone to the speaker, thumped it a couple of times on the dash for good measure, then snapped it shut and turned it off. I could kick myself for all the years I'd wasted resisting wireless technology.

THIRTY

Of course I didn't stop for lunch. I didn't even stop for a red light I could avoid without getting nailed. A box trap is no good if you aren't there in time to pull the string.

Iroquois Heights slumbered under the overcast, a tidy place of front porches, gift shops, homegrown restaurants named Welcome to Irene's and The Chef's Pantry, and no chain places inside the city limits because Irene and the chef had the council in their cash registers; no less a force of nature than Wal-Mart had been sandbagged in the middle of construction plans by pickets armed with preprinted signs. After it fled, the local shops went on charging triple for the same Chinese merchandise, and travelers who stopped to eat and fuel up in the neon belt of franchises that ringed the city seldom got a glimpse of what lay inside.

I serpentined the main stem as before and found an unmetered spot on a residential street around the corner from Iona's Simple Solutions. A city prowler crept past as I was locking up, both heads in the front seat turned toward the dinged and rusted sheetmetal; but it looked like rain, so the cop behind the wheel goosed the pedal and swung right at the corner. I resumed breathing and resettled the Luger on my belt so my coattail hung down straight over the butt.

Iona Ballista Cuneo sat at the C-shaped desk in the peach-colored reception room, holding a sleek telephone receiver to her ear and opening and closing drawers. The retro beehive went with the sleeveless sheath dress and a string of pearls: early Laura Petrie.

"I'm sorry," she said into the mouthpiece. "I can't find what she did with it. I'll call her at home. I left her in charge while I was in Beijing and I guess she took it upon herself to reorganize." She said good-bye, hung up, and smiled at me. "I've found it's easier to blame the help when something is misfiled. People expect perfection at the top. Are you making any progress on Joey's case?"

"Enough to know Marcine's not the help. You could've saved me some running around if you'd told me she was your partner when I was here before. I just came from Joey's."

That threw her for only a second. "I didn't know about the money, and I lived there; but of course he kept me a virgin from the business, not like Marcine. It was her idea to keep it just between us. Joey would've looked bad if anyone got curious and dug into the source of her capital. In his world, it's better to make up a loss out of your own pocket than be made the goat. Less fatal all around. I'm surprised he told you."

"Did I hear you say Marcine isn't in today?"

"She took personal time. She earned it. It's an eighteen-hour day when there aren't two to share it, and I was out of the country for four. She's relaxing at home. She certainly is popular today. Your boss asked about her too."

"My boss."

"Client; whatever euphemism you're most comfortable with. You and Lucille need to communicate better and avoid duplicating each other's efforts."

"When did she call?"

"She didn't call. She was here. I must say that in person she looks—"

"When?"

"Just now. Ten minutes ago. Is it important?"

I was pushing out through the air lock.

It might have been the state I was in, but the clouds seemed to hang lower over Ottawa Place than anywhere else, ramping up the atmospheric pressure and creating false twilight, pierced here and there by a lighted window or a light-sensitive lamp on a pole. The greenery had a grayish cast.

Not dark enough, though. Not by half if I wanted to sneak up on Marcine Logan's house unobserved. I decided against parking at the mouth of the cul-de-sac and drove right up to it.

I'd been so clever I'd outsmarted myself. Why not? It was my turn. I'd let Lucille think she had time to get there before me, and she'd turned out to be right. She did her own legal legwork and covered a territory larger than Rhode Island; she could have had any number of reasons for being in the vicinity.

Whatever. She'd pointed that Volvo of hers in this direction and here it was, snugged up to the curb in front of Marcine's house. I let my coat fall open and climbed the steps from the garage to the front door and rang the bell. The chimes echoed through the place like a pebble skipping across a bare floor, a lonely sound.

No one answered, and I didn't try again. The door was locked. I drew the pistol and used the butt to knock a diamond-shaped pane out of the rectangular strip of window to the right of the frame, reached in and around, found the dead bolt, and twisted it back. I hurled the door inward and went in big as Christmas. I wanted to draw her fire.

I didn't draw so much as a gasp. A shallow entryway opened into a great room that went straight up to the roof, where a stained-glass skylight on either side of the center beam broke the meager outside light into soft colors that fell on the floor. Furniture arrangements divided the room into a reading area, a grouping for conversation or watching television, and a portable bar. A floor and a table lamp with drum shades made golden pools on an oyster-colored carpet. I had all this to myself.

"Up here, Amos."

The room had good acoustics. I jumped as if she'd spoken in my ear. I looked up at a semicircular loft ringed with a railing of bright yellow brass. A large fixture, brass also, swayed slightly from a chain stapled to the center beam between the skylights. Three bulbs arranged like pawnshop globes burned in the center, their light deflected outward by the polished undersides of six petal-shaped shades.

"I can't see you, Lucille."

"I can see you, though. This chandelier makes a handy mirror. Marcine can stand here dripping from the shower and see who's come to call. Didn't help her this time, though. I'm a harmless-looking old frump until you get to know me."

"Where is she?"

"Here!" I heard the accent before one of Lucille's big hands choked it off.

"You lied to me," she said. "Not just about where you were when you called. I know Lee Tan's reputation. A call from Joey wouldn't spook her into giving up the woman who ratted him out. Finding God doesn't make you a coward. From what I hear it's just the opposite."

"I was improvising. I needed a reason to flush you out. I knew you knew about the call because you placed it." I tilted my head carefully. If she moved at all—if Marcine struggled and she had to react—I might see a reflection in the curved shades of the fixture. I didn't know if she had a gun on her or had tied her up.

"When did I do that?" Lucille asked.

"Just after that storm we had the other day. The lights went out and Lee checked to see if her niece had called to ask if she was okay."

"That's when. How about why?"

"To stir up dust. After you killed Frances Donella, you needed to draw the cops away from that investigation. They'd get a court order to look at Joey's telephone records, and when Lee Tan's number came up they'd question her. It wouldn't hurt Joey because she couldn't tell them anything. Meanwhile the Donella case would go stale, and they'd put it down to the hazards of streetwalking just to close it."

"So now I'm a strangler."

"You've got the build for it," I said, "and you'd know enough to wear gloves to keep from slashing up your hands. A dead snitch couldn't hurt Joey's defense."

The ceiling fixture had stopped swaying. The current of air I'd stirred when I threw open the door had settled. If I could kick it shut, I might start the chandelier swinging and catch Lucille's reflection. As things were I didn't know where to aim.

She said, "Sloppy, wasn't I? I picked the wrong girl."

"You're picking the wrong one now."

She said nothing. I kept talking, shifting my weight off my left foot. "Marcine didn't sell him to the cops. All she did was rip him off to buy a stake in Iona's shop. We'll never know who the real snitch was, if there was one. Severin wouldn't have been the first cop to invent a tip in order to get the warrants he needed. We can't ask him, can we?"

"Stop fidgeting, Amos. I'll shoot you where you stand. I'm an expert."

I stopped. I'd pushed it, moved my foot two inches when I should have settled for half. "I know. I saw the certificates on your office wall. Three-county champion, last year and this. I don't guess there's a self-defense course or an ex-cop you've missed. That was some score in Portage Lake, and with a forty-five."

"Severin, too? I guess Marcine would be the hat trick."

"Four, with me. You can't leave it there."

"Your math's better than your geography. You said Severin died during the storm, the same one that turned off Lee Tan's lights in Canton. How'd I call her from Joey's phone in Bloomingham when I was in Portage Lake killing Severin?"

"You palmed Joey's phone card when you found it under the phone in his living room."

"Nobody borrows phones anymore. We carry our own."

"Yours wouldn't work at his place. Mine wouldn't, either; it's a dead zone.

"Happy accident, for you," I said. "When you enter a code from a card, the billing number comes up on ID, no matter where you call from. It takes a cool hand to throw the cops off the trail of one murder just minutes after committing a second, but good lawyers don't rattle easily." I slid my foot a quarter-inch. That was a mistake.

Someone drew in a sharp breath. I froze.

"I've got a nine-millimeter under Marcine's chin," Lucille said. "Stay put or I'll drop the hammer."

"It's true!" Marcine sounded more than ever like Eliza Doolittle and less like Margaret Thatcher. She'd forgotten her upper-class accent.

I gave up my plan, relaxed my grip on the gun. My hand was sweating in the heat and slippery as an eel.

"You lost, Lucille. The verdict's in and you lost. You killed Donella for what she might have known that would tie your client to his first offense, then the arresting officer who could identify her as a witness. You planted the gun you used on him at Barry Stackpole's apartment so the cops would think he killed them both to keep Joey from beating the system. You plugged every hole. But the plugs won't hold if you kill Marcine."

The chandelier moved a centimeter. I hadn't stirred, and neither had the door. Something I'd said must have made Lucille jerk. I saw something reflected on the polished brass of one of the shades; part of a face, I thought. I tightened my grip and shifted the muzzle that direction. The image had been too brief. I couldn't be sure who I might hit.

"Yeah, it turned up," I said. "I found it. Your boy Bobby Lee got eager with the cue ball he used to coldcock him. A dead fall guy raises more questions than he answers."

"I don't know any Bobby Lee."

"You're not so good on the stand. A defendant makes an unconvincing witness when she's holding a pistol on someone. Anyway, he's using his one phone call to call you. That's why he ran the errand, wasn't it? You promised to represent him when his possession case went to trial."

"Let him squawk. There's nothing to tie that gun to me *or* Severin. The slug wasn't recovered."

"The shell casing was. You forgot to pick it up when you took Severin's cell and used it to call Lee Tan on Joey's card. Then you got rid of the cell, probably in the lake, so there'd be no record of where the call was actually placed.

"Joey did it, Lucille. He blamed the series of articles Barry was writing about his family for his mother's suicide. It's why he threatened Barry, and it's why he made good on it by planting dynamite in his car."

She sighed, a great gust of breath that set the fixture swinging again. I saw the scene then, in reflection: She had Marcine strapped to a straight chair in an open doorway belonging to an upstairs room and was crouched behind her and to her right holding a gray steel pistol—not under her chin now but pointing outward, with her other hand clamped over Marcine's mouth. From where I stood I could see the top of the doorway. I made another adjustment, carefully. I didn't want to startle her into turning that barrel back on her captive.

"I know it," Lucille said. "I've known it a long time."

"Joey told you?"

"Him? He'd lie in confession to get a writ from the priest. I told you I was hoping to track down that wad of gum the bomber used to paste down the wires. I didn't tell you I'd already found it."

"Where?"

"An evidence clerk took it home when the city condemned those two floors at Thirteen Hundred. He forgot to sign them out, and he forgot to bring them back after he retired."

"You're a good detective, Lucille. You didn't need me after all."

"Reliance found him, not me."

"I didn't read that in their report."

"I held back that page. I wanted to keep you on the scent. I told the clerk he'd lose his pension if I let it slip out he was guilty of obstruction. He bought me off cheap. He gave me a piece of gum.

"I got Joey to let me scrape a culture from inside his mouth and had the skin cells compared to the dried saliva on the piece at a private lab. They never ask questions, and they don't keep copies of the results. My clients pay for that. It was a solid match. I destroyed the report along with the gum."

"When did you get the results?"

She chuckled, dry as paint peeling in an acetylene flame. "The day I hired you. You were wrong, Amos; I did need you. I needed you to point me where I had to go."

I fired then. I was planning to anyway.

THIRTY-ONE

I aimed for the architecture, my only sure shot. A piece of wood jumped out of the top of the doorframe, leaving a yellow scar. I was moving by then.

She returned fire. I didn't hear the slug strike in the echo of the two blasts, but I felt the impact through the floor the instant after I landed on my shoulder. I rolled up onto my feet and made for the bottom step of a staircase upholstered in the same oyster-colored pile that covered the floor, bounded over it and hit every third step going up. I avoided the side railed in brass; if she snapped one down the staircase that was the direction she'd pick. That was my second mistake in five minutes.

The inside wall was finished in textured plaster. It exploded, spraying chalk in my face. I'd seen a flash of movement at the top just in time to avoid running into a bullet, which pierced the air where my head would have been if I'd taken the next step. I fired from reflex, but she was gone by then and I hadn't had time to aim. Brass rang.

Silence then, or what passed for it. A plane could have

crashed through the second story and I wouldn't have heard it for the ringing in my ears.

My eyes were filled with tears and dust. I backed down several steps to clear them with a sleeve. For a second I was a fat target, but Lucille was being cautious now after two misses. I was going to have to come to her.

That was the last thing I wanted to do. I thought about calling for backup. My cell was on my front passenger seat, where I'd tossed it after talking to Alderdyce. I might as well have left it with a duck on a firing range.

I wanted to stay on that staircase. I'd stayed in places a lot less comfortable. I hadn't the luxury to choose. Lucille had a hostage and I was responsible for that.

I resumed climbing, slow as the hands on a clock. I was leaning on the railing now. It made a swell slide if I had to retreat in a hurry. Four steps from the top I got down on my hands and knees and crawled, an awkward position with a gun in one fist, but if she was waiting for me around the corner the odds were she'd be aiming at trunk level. That's what they teach when you take a firearms course designed for your protection. Legs are too hard to hit.

But this was Lefty Lucy, who seldom played by the rules.

Out of the tail of my eye I saw a face where a face couldn't exist. It startled me, and I almost went into a flat slide down the steps. My head was level with the bottom of the hanging light fixture, and in the polished curve of one shade I saw Lucille's profile from the waist up. She wasn't wearing one of her usual blazers and the gray steel of her semiautomatic extended at a downward angle from a stiff arm in a white sleeve, supported by her other hand around her wrist. She was standing eight feet from the top of the stairs aiming just above the floor.

She'd picked her spot with care. The fixture reflected the upper part of the stairs, and if I were ascending them the customary way she'd see me in it.

Trust her to choose another head shot.

I felt like a bug in a jar. Then I realized it wasn't me in the jar. I could see her, but as long as I stayed down I was invisible. Not that it solved any problems. The only way I could crawl was backward, and that moved Marcine back to the top of the target list. When Lucille realized I wasn't coming she'd shoot the bird in hand before she went looking for the one in the bush.

"Lucille?"

The tricky acoustics rattled her. Her head moved, glancing around. I might have been standing next to her in the loft. She relaxed her stance a little.

"I'm here, Amos. Where are you?" Her eyes pawed the mirrored shades.

"I just wanted to say that after you kill us, you'll still be in trouble with the Internal Revenue Service. They never back off."

"Funny. I knew I made a mistake when I sent you after those computer files. I should've let them go and sued to get them back. I could make a case against having them admitted on the grounds they were illegally obtained."

"Well, you had a lot on your mind."

"So do you. I'm going to kill your little English toffee if you keep me waiting."

"How do I know you didn't? She's been pretty quiet, and I lost track of the shots."

"I gagged her. She's got some mouth on her when she's not playing Princess Di."

While we were talking I gathered my legs under me and got a grip on the railing. A board creaked under the carpeting. She sent a glance toward the fixture, then returned her concentration to the top of the stairs, the gun slanting down.

I pulled myself up all of a piece and took the rest of the steps in one bound. My reflection flashing in the brass shade distracted her. Her head jerked that way, but her finger was still on the trigger. Both guns went off at once.

THIRTY-TWO

We were in a different waiting room in the same hospital: Inspector John Alderdyce, U.S. Marshal Mary Ann Thaler, and me. Lieutenant Hornet was out browsing a snack machine. The nurse was going to come get us when she finished changing Barry's sheets.

"I appreciate the invitation, Inspector," Thaler said. "The only federal charges involved are the FBI's department, not mine."

"Call me John. We're equals now. You may have the edge. I knew you were interested, and I know about that other thing. It's also the reason I'm doing this." He took the hefty manila envelope he'd been resting his hands on in his lap and tossed it at me. I almost fell out of my chair catching it. I opened the flap and looked at the file he'd used to pressure me.

A blush looked good on Thaler. Anything would. A while back we'd conspired to save Alderdyce's job. He wasn't supposed to know about it, but a big city is a small town really.

"I'll regret that," he said to me. "You damn near got three people killed on top of the two we already had in a drawer."

"I had to flush her out, John. I didn't mean to cut it that close, but once an amateur tastes blood twice it gets easier the third time."

"Don't call me John."

"What's in the envelope?" Thaler asked.

"Walker's balls, I thought. He might as well have 'em back for all the good they did me. I'm starting a new file."

We'd moved to Barry's floor after Lucille Lettermore went into recovery from surgery. My bullet had nicked the spleen but she was expected to be well enough to attend her first arraignment in a wheelchair. By the time all the charges were read she could be in training for the Olympics.

Her marksmanship hadn't fallen off after Severin. The bullet shattered the floor where she'd been aiming when I shot her. Her pistol fell when she did and I kicked it out of the loft and went to see about Marcine Logan. Lucille had tied her to the vanity chair in her dressing room with the sash from a bathrobe, the first thing she could grab when she saw me drive up. Marcine was dressed for a day at home, barefoot in jeans and an old fitted shirt worn tail out. She had a mouth on her when I got the twist of towel off her face, the lawyer hadn't lied about that.

I'd spent an ugly couple of hours with the police in Iroquois Heights, but Alderdyce had pried me loose there. The lieutenant in charge of the investigation was only one promotion away from getting booted out with the current administration and had asked about opportunities in Detroit.

My cell rang. It was Lee Tan the Younger. "I haven't a thing in my refrigerator. How about buying me dinner?"

I told her to hang on. "Am I in custody?"

Alderdyce said, "Check the file."

I got it out and opened it to the back. All three copies of the Iroquois Heights arrest report were there.

"Now you owe me."

"Pick you up at eight," I told Lee.

"Why don't I drive? You sound beat."

"Not on your life." I rang off. "How's Bobby Lee?"

Alderdyce rolled his big shoulders. "Still shot, but that's the least of his worries. It's back to the public defender for him. You made a lucky guess on those Columbine wannabes; Lucy was a paid consultant. That establishes opportunity to obtain the forty-five. Strike pattern on the shell at the marina matched up. You should be ashamed of yourself. The hospital's running out of beds."

"I hear Joey Ballistic's in Beaumont."

"In the basement," he said. "He had a second heart attack when they were wheeling him into the OR. Tell Stackpole when you see him. It's better than flowers."

I hoped Dr. Nagler didn't fudge on the certificate of death. I'd sort of liked him.

I asked Alderdyce where Barry stood.

"Prosecutor's talking plea deal with Bobby Lee's P.D. if he'll testify she put the forty-five in his hand. That establishes chain of possession and clears Stackpole. We may never tie her to Frances Donella; but you can only serve one life sentence."

"She'll never see trial. All those high-test cases fried her brains in the end."

"That's when her troubles begin. Tax hounds don't care how looney you are as long as you pay up. Speaking of them," he said, "your statement's mushy on that point."

"I'd tell you, but I'd be starting a new tab."

Thaler crossed her legs in her chair. She had on a tan tailored suit with a slit in the skirt that broke just above the knee. "Stupid business. Two dead, three in the hospital, and a career in pieces over a hoodlum who should never have been let out of jail in the first place, and then he ups and dies."

"Tell me about it," I said. "I have to stand in line behind Washington just to sue for expenses."

Alderdyce watched me. "The left-handed dollar, that all you think about?"

"Keeps my mind off my sore jaw."

The nurse came in, a short stocky veteran of drive-bys and arson victims with kind eyes in a face blasted from granite. "One at a time, please. Mr. Stackpole has to have rest if he's going to give up his bed to someone who needs it." She looked from one face to another. "Who's first?"

I tucked the envelope under my arm and got up to visit my friend.

ABOUT THE AUTHOR

Loren D. Estleman has written more than sixty novels. He has already netted four Shamus Awards for detective fiction, five Spur Awards for Western fiction, and three Western Heritage Awards, among his many professional honors. He has written many Amos Walker mysteries, *The Left-Handed Dollar* being the twentieth. He lives with his wife, author Deborah Morgan, in Michigan.